Hello, Bob!

Enjoy it in good health.

David Etter

7/12/09

A Bag of Gold

A Novel

By

David Estes

Eloquent Books
New York, New York

Eloquent Books
An imprint of AEG Publishing Group
845 Third Avenue, 6th Floor - 6016
New York, NY 10022
www.eloquentbooks.com

ISBN: 978-1-60860-086-1
SKU: 1-60860-086-6

Printed in the United States of America

Book Layout by: Roger Hayes

Cover Design by: Ron Peterman

A Bag of Gold

One

Aubrey Roan slung five slugs from his Colt's .44 into the back bar mirror of the Black Hawk Saloon.

"Aubrey, you drunk bastard!" Ned Toomey, the bartender, screamed. "What the hell are you doing?"

Just then Marshal Joe Freeman's stocky frame split the batwings.

"Roan!" Freeman yelled.

Roan lit out the back way and headed for the livery stable.

Freeman took out after him. He got there in time to see Roan mounting his big roan stallion.

"Hold it right there, Roan!" the marshal shouted.

"Give it up, Joe," Roan sneered. He whipped out his gun and ripped a slug into Freeman's chest.

Freeman fell dead in the stench of the soured hay and horse manure covering the stable floor.

Roan struck a match and tossed it onto a pile of loose straw. The straw flared, and the flames spread like water on a flat rock, licking at the tinder dry walls. Roan watched with a satisfied smirk.

Golly Moses, the stable owner, was napping in a nearby stall. He was jarred awake by the gunshot, smelled smoke and began a frantic search for the source of the odor. He spotted the broad rump of Roan's stallion hightailing it out the back door of the stable.

"Fire!" Moses screamed.

The flames were already climbing the stable walls.

Moses grabbed a bucket and headed for the water tank. He stumbled over the body of the dead marshal. Golly flung the bucket aside, laid hold of Freeman's body, and started dragging it from the flaming building.

"Fire, dammit, fire!" he yelled.

People poured out of saloons and swarmed to where the fire was lighting up the sky. Around the corner the horse-drawn fire wagon reeled with excited dogs nipping at the heels of the frenzied steeds.

A man grabbed hold of Freeman's body and helped Moses drag it clear of the burning building.

"What happened?" the man said.

"Damned if I know," Moses said. "I heard a shot and smelled smoke, then I seen the marshal sprawled out on the floor deader'n a doornail."

"It must have been that Roan fellow."

"It was him all right. Damn fool ought to be strung up by his thumbs."

Two

Will Savage plunked along the boardwalk, stewing over the session he'd just had with Lester Hogan, president of the Bank of Junction City.

"We're calling your loan, Savage," Hogan had said.

Hogan was a scrawny little weasel of a man. Shaggy gray hair covered his huge ears. Crowding the middle of his craggy face was a bulbous nose, red as a circus clown's.

"Calling my loan?" Savage couldn't believe it. "It's still got eight months to go."

Hogan surveyed the lean, thin-faced cowman glaring down at him from the other side of the desk. The banker blew his nose into a fist, licked his palm, then wiped it on his shirt.

Savage winced.

"We've got a new board coming in," Hogan whined, "and we need to show them a strong capital base. Make us look good for the auditors. Know what I mean, Savage?"

"Auditors be damned," Savage said. "We had a deal. I've never missed an interest payment."

"Been a while, though, since you paid anything on the principal." Hogan fingered the gray stubble on his chin. "I need a thousand dollars by the first of September, or the board will be forced to foreclose on you."

Savage eyed him with a vengeance. Hogan had wanted his range for years, and Savage knew it. In normal times, when the rains came when they were supposed to, his was the best grazing land in the county. Hogan had tried to use the bad times to force him to sell, but so far, Savage had been able to block his move.

Now, Hogan had a new scheme, using the board as a lever, betting that Savage wouldn't be able to raise the thousand dollars in time to meet the deadline.

Hogan's plot was not lost on Savage.

"That's less than a month away," he said.

"Ain't much I can do. The board—"

"Don't lay it off on the board, Les."

Savage struggled to keep from grabbing the banker by the collar and wiping that smirk off his face.

"Everybody knows you call the shots around here," Savage said.

"Well, we all have to answer to somebody, don't we?"

"You know as well as I do the grass is burned up, and the cattle market has gone to hell."

Savage wasn't happy, and he showed it He leaned across the desk, eyeball-to-eyeball with the lecherous banker.

"What happened to the money you said would always be there if I needed it?"

"Ain't the same world we're living in today, Savage. Things are different here in 1883 than they were five-ten years ago. A handshake don't mean the same no more."

Hogan stood up, letting Savage know the conversation was over.

"Money's tighter these days," he said. "Times have changed." He emphasized that by saying it again. "Times have changed."

Savage nodded

"Uh-huh," he said. "So have people." He turned on a heel and left the banker staring at his back.

Clomping in deep thought past Alec Bean's barber shop, Savage heard Alec pecking on his window. The barber motioned him inside.

Savage stuck his head in the door.

"Howdy, Alec."

Alec was snipping at a napping man's hair.

"Some fellow was in here looking for you," said the bald barber.

"He better find me fast. I'm heading out."

"Said he had a message for you from a judge in Abilene."

"Well, I don't know any judge in Abilene," Savage said. "If he wants to see me, I'll be at my place."

Three

On top of a bald knob overlooking his squalling herd, Savage sat his sorrel mare, making a head count. With Hogan breathing down his neck he had to find a way to get out from under his loan at the bank.

The last thing he wanted was to see his ranch fall into the clutches of the greedy banker. Still, the way things were, even if he sold the herd, he wasn't sure it would bring enough to save his ranch. The hard truth was, if he sold the herd, it would take years to build another one. Maybe he'd be smart to sell out, pay off his debt, and start over someplace else. Ben Cassidy had been at him to come back to work for him at the Cattleman's Association.

That thought lasted about as long as it took to think it. He tossed it aside. His range detective days were long gone. He was a cattleman now.

Savage was curious as to what the man from Abilene had in mind, but he had no time to waste jawing with a judge he didn't know. Chances were he wanted him to go chasing after some hombre the law couldn't find, and Savage didn't have time for that. Anyway, if he tracked the outlaw down, somebody likely would have to die, and Savage wasn't ready for it to be him.

Only half the sun was sticking up behind the parched, low-lying hills, and thin fingers of orange and red streaked across the western sky. Outlined against it, Savage saw a shadow moving his way. A man on horseback.

Rain-thirsty sedge grass brushed the belly of the rider's dun gelding.

"Howdy," the man said from behind a scraggly red beard. "My name's Amos Cully."

"Will Savage."

"Feller in town said I'd find you here," Cully said with a grin. "Judge Barker in Abilene sent me to tell you he'd like to talk to you."

"Judge Barker?"

"Judge Owen J. Barker."

The name didn't ring any bells.

"It's a long ride to Abilene for a chat," Savage said.

"I know the judge. He wouldn't ask you to ride plum out there on no wild goose chase."

"Do you know what it's about?"

"I know. They's money in it. But I think the judge would ruther talk to you about it hisself."

Savage's ears perked up. What kind of money? And for doing what? He squinted into the sun. Not much of it left. Darkness would bring his cattle some relief from the heat, but streams were running low, and the near empty ponds had been stagnant for weeks. Only the turtles had survived.

A ride to Abilene might be worth it. It wouldn't cost him anything but time, which he didn't have a lot of.

Cully hadn't said how much money was in it, if he knew. But, Savage decided that if there was a chance a talk with the judge could save his ranch, he'd have to take it.

"All right," he said. "You tell the judge I'll be out there to see him."

"I'll do that. Reckon you'd be able to get away the next day or two?"

"Is he in a hurry?"

"I reckon not. Just figgered he'd like to know when to start looking for you."

"It's a couple of days ride to Abilene. Tell him I'll be leaving here the day after tomorrow."

"That's what I'll tell him." Cully touched a finger to his hat, and gigged his gelding west.

"Be seeing you, Savage."

Four

Golly Moses looked up from the pile of ashes and watched the leisurely approach of a stranger on horseback. Strangers usually piqued his curiosity, but now, he went back to poking around in the ash heap that once was his livery stable.

"All I had in the world," he grumbled. "Got to find some way to build it back."

A gaunt man in dingy blue pants with red suspenders, Golly rubbed a gnarled fist against his unshaven chin, scratched his hairy gray neck, and squinted at the stranger.

The lanky rider pulled up beside the query-eyed stable master who greeted him with a silent stare.

The stranger nodded toward the ash heap.

"Your place?" he said.

"It was my place 'fore that damn fool put a match to it," Moses spat. "You think I'd be pokin' around in a heap of ashes that never belonged to me?"

The stranger grinned.

"I'm Will Savage," he said. "I'm supposed to see a Judge Barker."

"You a friend of his?"

"He sent for me."

13

Moses stuck out a hand. "I'm Golly Moses, Mr. Savage," he said. "I never meant to be so uppity, but this stable belonged to me, and that dang fool burnt it down."

Savage gave him a sympathetic nod

"Can you tell me where I'll find the judge?"

"You betcha." Moses pointed down the street. "See that big building down yonder on the right side of the street? That's the bank. You go on past there about ten steps and you'll come to a hallway that takes you back to a big old door with the judge's name on it. You can't miss it."

"Thanks. Good luck with your livery."

Savage gigged the mare toward the false-front building that Moses pointed out. He swung out of the saddle and dropped a rein over the hitch rail, and stretched the trail weariness out of his bones. An instinctive look around told him there was nothing unusual about the horses and wagons lining both sides of the street. He moved inside the building, and his dusty boots made muffled thuds on the wooden floor of the shadowy hallway.

He found the big oak door that Moses said would be there with the judge's name on it. HONORABLE OWEN J. BARKER. Savage wondered why judges' names were preceded by "honorable." He had known some who weren't.

"Come in!" was the brusque response to his knock.

Savage pushed the door open.

Behind a huge mahogany desk sat a bald man about sixty years old, puffing on a corncob pipe, fussing with papers strewn on the desk. Without looking up, the judge waved Savage to a cane-bottom chair. Savage sat on it.

While he waited, Savage's eyes roamed around the room. The walls were lined with shelves from floor to ceiling. The shelves were loaded with heavy books, most of which Savage thought would make good doorstops. After a few minutes, he cleared his throat to remind the judge that he was there.

"Confounded red tape!" the judge roared. "A man could get buried in this stuff."

"You sent for me, judge?"

"Are you Savage?"

"I'm Savage."

Barker's head came up, and he faced the sun-leathered cowboy on the other side of his desk.

"Then I sent for you," he said.

The judge put a match to his pipe, puffed a few times until the cloud of smoke grew big enough to suit him.

"I suppose you have no idea why you're here," he said.

"Two days ago a man named Amos Cully looked me up and said you wanted to talk to me."

With a practiced eye, Judge Barker made a quick survey of the man he had summoned for a job that he couldn't do himself. He noted the unwavering pale blue eyes, thin lips that curled up at the corners, firm square jaw, and long-fingered hands that looked like they weren't afraid of work.

"I hear you're good at finding people," the judge said.

Here it comes, Savage told himself.

"I've found some," he said.

"A while back a man named Joe Freeman was shot and killed at the livery stable here in Abilene. Freeman was the town marshal. He did a lot of good for this town, as good a lawman as we ever had. He restored law and order, made Abilene livable again after those wild days."

Savage listened. He had heard enough to get an idea of where the judge's story was going.

He'd heard it before in different forms from different people. Some renegade was cross ways with the law, and the judge hadn't been able to run him down. He'd learned of Savage's reputation as a range detective, and was making his case.

The judge was still talking.

"It turns out Freeman was something else too. I'll tell you about that in a minute. Somewhere there's a man named Aubrey Roan who we believe killed Freeman. Roan was a troublemaker, and had been involved in several scrapes before. He took off for the livery stable after some disturbance, and Freeman went after him. My guess is that tempers flared, things got out of hand, and Roan shot him. He wouldn't have had the stomach to face Freeman in a fair fight.

"We know now that there was a price on Freeman's head. Some old charge from years ago out west. Two-thousand-dollar reward for him dead or alive. Word got back to them that Freeman was dead, and they contacted me. Needless to say, this town was shocked."

Barker pulled open a desk drawer and brought out a small leather pouch tied with a drawstring.

"I have to tell you, Savage," he said with a steady gaze, "if Roan was here now, I'd be tempted to do to him what he did to Joe Freeman. I don't know what Joe did out west, but in Abilene he was nothing but good. He didn't deserve what he got from that hothead." He tossed the bag onto the desk. "In that bag is a thousand dollars in gold. That's half of what the law says Roan is entitled to for killing Freeman. I don't have the man power to go chasing after him, so, if you can locate Roan, and deliver this bag of gold to him, the other half is yours."

Savage let that soak in. Roan was to be rewarded for killing a lawman who had a price on his head? What about the charge against Roan? It didn't smell right.

Still, across his mind flashed a painful reminder of a herd of cattle that he was in danger of losing. With the judge's thousand dollars he could keep Hogan from stealing his land.

"What about the charge against Roan?" he said.

Barker dismissed that with a wave of his hand.

"That's a bridge we'll have to cross when we get to it. And we will get to it."

Savage didn't push it. He figured the judge was the judge, and whatever he did may not be honorable, but it would be legal.

"I like your forthrightness, Savage. Ben Cassidy over at the Cattleman's Association remembered you from a few years back. He said you were the man for the job, and I'm glad we got together. Twenty years ago I'd have taken that ride to Buffalo Flats myself, but not today."

"Buffalo Flats?" Savage was surprised at the excitement he heard in his own voice.

"That's somewhere west of Wichita."

Savage knew where it was. He and Carrie had lived near Buffalo Flats when they were married twelve years ago. That was where he had lost her to Denver Dunn. A bitter memory.

"Is that where I'll find Roan?" he said.

"The last we knew he was headed that way."

The judge stood up and walked around his desk. He placed a hand under Savage's elbow and steered him toward the door.

"Find Roan for me, Will," he said. "I can't close the book on this case until the reward has been delivered."

Savage took the hand that Barker extended.

"When will I hear from you?" the judge said.

"When I make up my mind."

Barker blinked and watched him go.

On his way out, Savage was greeted by a sea of bawling, restless longhorns pushing their way down the middle of Texas Street. Up the Chisholm Trail they had struggled, across Oklahoma Territory, and on to the railhead at Abilene. Whooping drovers urged their thirsty, heat-irritated charges toward the Great Western stock pens east of town. In Kansas a steer was worth thirty dollars, compared to four in Texas. Since 1867, upwards of three million head had been shipped from Abilene to the eastern markets.

Savage ducked into the Bull's Head Saloon and ordered whiskey. He sipped at it, killing time, waiting for the commotion on the street to settle, so he could find a place to eat and bed down for the night.

"Soul-searching time, Savage?"

Savage squared around and saw Amos Cully grinning up at him.

"Cully!" he said, glad to see a friendly face.

"It's a long ride from Junction City, ain't it?" Cully said.

"Long and hot."

Cully had a hand wrapped around a glass of beer, half way to his mustache-covered lips.

"You see the judge?" he said.

"I saw him."

"'Pears to me you made the right decision."

"How's that?"

"Be damned if I'd do that job. A man would have to be plum loco, riding to hell and gone all by hisself, toting a bag of gold. Ain't no secret the judge has been trying to smoke out Aubrey Roan. You ain't the first one he asked for help."

"Is that so? Did he ask you?"

"Be damned if he'd ask me! I reckon he knew I wouldn't have went."

"Why not?"

Cully sipped at his beer.

"Money ain't no good if you ain't alive to spend it," he said.

"There's something to that." Savage gave his left ear lobe a thoughtful tug. "Is that why the others turned him down?"

Cully nodded. "Ain't no telling how many knows about that reward money—good and bad. More people knows, more likely a feller could get hisself dead for it. Hear what I'm saying, Savage?"

Savage pointed his glass at the skinny, sleeve-gartered bartender and watched him refill it.

"Do you know this Roan fellow, Amos?"

"Never knew him. Seen him around. He rides a big old roan stallion. Strange acting hombre. Eyes ain't never still." He grinned. "St. Vita's dance or something. You wouldn't catch me turning my back on him, that's for dang sure.

"See, Savage, Roan knows he killed Freeman. Every time he hears that name—gold or no—he's gonna believe he's being brought in for Joe's killing, and he'll run like a rabbit at a hound dog convention."

Savage bottomed-up his glass. "How come you rode all the way out to Junction City to tell me the judge wanted to see me?"

"Money. I do jobs like that for the judge sometimes. He pays me good for what I do."

18

"Uh-huh. Well, old timer, good luck to you. Maybe our trails will cross again sometime."

"If you decide to go," Cully said—and Savage wondered how Cully knew he hadn't decided already—"a man like me could be a heap of help to you."

"I expect you could."

Savage tossed some coins on the bar, and made a move to leave, then stopped.

"Amos," he said.

"Yeah, Will?"

"You wouldn't be setting me up so you could get your hands on that reward money, would you?"

"Be damned if I would, Savage!"

"That's more money than you could make doing a dozen jobs for the judge, I imagine."

"Well, yeah, but—"

"I'll keep you in mind."

Savage elbowed his way through the crowd of punchers and headed for the batwing doors on his way out.

"Savage!"

He heard Cully call, but kept moving.

"You ain't got no idee who your friends is," Cully shouted at his back, "till you need 'em real bad."

Five

Oil lamps cast flickering images on the walls along the street as Savage headed toward the Drover's Cottage Inn. From the stock pens he heard the squalls of restless cattle. Sounds of laughter and loud talk spilled from the saloons onto the night air.

"Hey there, Mr. Will Savage."

Savage recognized the gaunt figure of Golly Moses limping toward him in the shadows.

"If I was you," Moses said, "I'd be mighty careful walking around out here in the dark all by myself."

"How so?"

"Lots of folks would kill for that kind of money." Golly seemed anxious to be some place else. "The whole town knows you been talking to the judge."

Savage took a cautious look around.

"Thanks for the warning," he said, though he had already thought of that.

He moved on, thinking less of his safety than of Aubrey Roan and Judge Barker.

He rounded the corner to the Drover's and some hooligan leaped out of the shadows and onto his back. Savage grabbed him by the collar and flung him over his head and onto the gravel street. Savage pounced on him and pinned him to the ground. Another ruffian bashed him from behind with a double-fisted blow to the head. Dazed, Savage felt groping hands rifling through his pockets.

"It ain't here," he heard a coarse voice complain. "He ain't got it!"

"Let's get the hell out of here," said another.

Savage dragged himself to his feet and shook his head clear. He brushed himself off and headed for the Drover's. Cully's words rang loud and clear: No telling how many knows about this—good and bad.

He would have some questions for the judge when he saw him tomorrow morning.

Judge Barker greeted him outside his office door. Savage thought he acted like he was in some kind of tizzy.

"Would you mind waiting here for a moment, Savage?" the judge said. "I've got some people in my office, and I'd rather not disturb the meeting."

Barker disappeared through the big oak door.

The shiny brass letters spelling out the judge's name glared at the musing Savage. He was not going to let the judge railroad him into doing something he didn't feel right about. He wasn't eager to go chasing after some yahoo who had already had plenty of time to be some place else by the time he got there. On the other hand, he had about used up all his choices. This one might be his last.

The door flew open, and the judge stood in it. In his hand he held the little bag of gold that he had shown Savage the day before.

"I'm pleased that you decided to answer my call for help, Will."

"Judge, there's a thing or two that we need to talk about. Now, right off—"

From the other side of the door, an urgent voice called, "We're waiting, Judge Barker."

Barker shoved the bag of gold into Savage's hand, and said, "Have a safe trip, Will."

He hurried back inside and closed the door behind him.

21

Savage stood for a moment, studying the leather pouch, bouncing it in his palm. He questioned whether going after Roan was the wise thing to do.

Yet, he couldn't shake the image of Lester Hogan sitting back there in his bank, grinning like a Cheshire cat, betting he wouldn't come up with the money in time to save his ranch.

That ranch meant more than anything to him.

Except for Carrie.

From somewhere in the shadowy corners of his mind emerged the real reason he was anxious to hit the trail to Buffalo Flats. To find Carrie.

Six

Savage mounted the wooden steps to Blanchard's General Store, and reviewed the list of what he needed for the trip west: Jerky, coffee, beans and tobacco. While other customers sought the attention of the freckle-faced young man behind the counter, Savage went about gathering up his own items.

He had been there before. The first time was twelve years ago, when he first laid eyes on Carrie Ames. He had just ridden up from Texas with a herd from the Short "T" outfit. An October breeze kicked up, and he decided he had better be buying some warn underwear. Carrie was a clerk at Blanchard's. From the moment he saw her, Will was stricken with her youthful beauty and friendly manner.

Carrie was eighteen at the time. Will was seven years older, built like an oak plank, and shy as a lamb at a coyote wedding. Captivated by the vivacious Carrie, it took him a week to work up the gumption to ask her to supper. A week after that, he asked her to marry him. He was shocked when she said yes.

"I'd be proud to be Mrs. Will Savage," she said.

On a Sunday afternoon, in the front parlor of Carrie's Aunt Lou, Will and Carrie became man and wife. They moved onto land near Buffalo Flats that Will bought from a land agent.

Savage placed his items on the counter in front of the freckle-faced clerk and waited for him to tally them up.

"What else can I get for you?" the young man said.

"That ought to do it," Will said.

"You've got enough stuff here for a barn-raising."

"Nope. Just a few days' ride." He checked his bill, and said with a frown, "Has the price gone up on jerky?"

"Beans. All the way up to a nickel a pound."

Savage shook his head. He couldn't believe how the price of everything kept going up. He paid his bill and took up the brown paper sack.

He placed the provisions in the saddlebags and climbed into the saddle for the long ride. He twisted a jaw full of tobacco from the plug of Red Star, and reined the mare toward Buffalo Flats.

"Come on, horse," he said. "Let's go get it done."

Seven

Slashes of late afternoon sunlight slithered through the cottonwoods, slicing the lengthening shadows. For five days, heavy, merciless heat had hovered over the plains of western Kansas. Savage felt like he had been squeezed through a gun barrel. Five days of brow-swiping with a sweat-soaked bandanna had taken their toll.

Spurring the mare to a gentle trot, he calculated that one more day should get him to Buffalo Flats. He looked forward to a glass of cold beer that he could almost feel trickling down into his innards, forcing the pain from his body, even as his sweaty blue cotton shirt clung to him like mud to a wagon bed.

He never knew it to be so hot, not even in the drought of '77 when old timers swore it was "hotter than hell had any right to be." Streams dried up, and cattle died for lack of water. Will had borrowed money to tide him over until times got better. They only got worse. He was finally forced to sell out to pay off his loan. He didn't want that to happen again.

His land gone, he had hired out as an Army scout, hunted buffalo for the hides, then signed on as a range detective for the Cattleman's Association.

At one time, he had freighted supplies to miners in the Dakota hills with a man named Denver Dunn. On the way to a mining camp with a shipment of provisions, he and Dunn were attacked by a band of renegade Sioux. Savage caught an arrow in the stomach. Writhing in pain, he hurtled from his mount.

Dunn scrambled for cover in a nearby ravine, and made no attempt to help his wounded partner. He stayed out of sight until the Sioux rode away with the loaded wagon. Dunn then took off on Savage's horse, and never came back.

A cavalry patrol in pursuit of the Sioux, found Savage and removed him to the infirmary at Fort Waring. Weeks of recovery from surgery made him determined to get back to Carrie. As soon as he could ride, he lit out for Buffalo Flats. He found Carrie in a small cabin on the edge of town, married to Denver Dunn. Dunn had convinced Carrie that Savage died in the Sioux raid, and talked her into marrying him.

Stunned by Carrie's shouting, "We're going to have a baby—a baby you said could wait!" Savage rode away without a backward glance.

Even so, the nagging need to know whether she was still in Buffalo Flats would not let go.

Maybe tomorrow he would find out.

He urged the mare toward the low-lying hills in the distance. The sun was settling behind them. One more day to Buffalo Flats. He would smoke out Aubrey Roan, hand over the bag of gold, and high-tail it back to Abilene for his pay from Judge Barker. With the thousand dollars, he would rescue his ranch from Lester Hogan and be home free.

That was his plan. He was yet to learn, however, of Henry Wadsworth whose mother would die in his arms; the Barefoot clan hell-bent to shed Savage's blood for "killing our kin;" and John Castledine, town marshal at Buffalo Flats, who was Roan's brother.

Eight

The shadows deepened into dusk, and from dusk to darkness. Savage figured it was time he got some rest for his last day's ride to Buffalo Flats. He found a small stream that was still trickling, and tethered the mare nearby so she could water and nibble at the sparse grass.

While the coffee brewed over a small fire, he chomped down a fistful of jerky. When the coffee had boiled long enough to suit him, he poured himself a tin cup full and settled back against his saddle. Before the cup was empty, he was asleep.

The snap of a dry twig popped Savage's eyes wide open. His fingers closed around the butt of the Colt's .45 strapped to his thigh.

In the glow of the campfire stood a gray horse. Atop the horse sat a gray haired man with gloved hands stacked on the pummel. His eyes fixed on Savage, across his thin lips sneaked an impish grin.

"Are you looking for somebody, mister?" Savage said.

"I saw the fire," said the stranger with a voice that sounded like it had escaped from the bowels of a gravel pit. "I figured if I rode in I'd be less likely to get shot than if I tried to be quiet about it."

Savage moved to a sitting position, getting a good look at the crease-browed rider.

The man's grin got wider.

"Mind if I step down?" he said.

Savage relaxed his grip on the .45.

"Go ahead."

The stranger swung down, and squatted on his heels beside the fire.

"My name's Jim Whitley," he said. "We might be able to help each other."

"How's that?"

"You asked if I was looking for somebody. The answer is yes. Word back in Abilene is that you're looking for the same man."

"Is that so?"

"A man named Aubrey Roan."

Savage got interested. "What about Roan?"

"I've been trailing you for about a week to ask you that question."

"How did you know about me?"

"Word gets around. There aren't many secrets out here when money's involved." He paused, and took a deep breath. "You haven't told me, but I know you're Will Savage. I understand you're after this Roan fellow to pay him for killing Marshal Joe Freeman."

"That's right."

"Some folks think Roan should hang for that killing, instead of being paid for it."

"Does that include you, Mr. Whitley?"

"It does."

Savage gave that a thoughtful moment.

"Where do you fit in?" he said.

"We've had several lawmen shot and killed in recent years by renegades like Roan. Because of that, some influential people have got together and formed the Lawman's Protective Association. I work for the Association. My job is to round up these killers and bring them back to stand trial." Again he paused, leaned closer across the fire, and pinned Savage with a steady gaze.

"I've got five hundred dollars that says you'll find Aubrey Roan. If you bring him back, the five hundred is yours."

Savage didn't need to think about that. He could have used the five hundred, but he had already made a deal with Judge Barker.

"I can't do that, Mr. Whitley."

"Maybe if you gave it a little thought it might look different to you."

"I'm afraid not. My deal is with Judge Barker in Abilene. I can't pay a man with one hand and collect on him with the other."

Whitley knew the conversation was over.

"Well, I sure do appreciate your honesty, Savage. Like the Good Book says, a man can't serve two masters."

Whitley swung into the saddle. "I thought you might save me a long ride," he said, "but I guess I'll be taking this one after all." He touched the brim of his hat in a parting salute. "I'd be mighty careful out here if I were you. We're not the only ones who know about that reward money."

With that he wheeled the gray about and disappeared beyond a stand of Osage orange.

The first light of dawn filtered through the sycamores. Somewhere in the distance Savage heard the yip-yip of a hungry coyote in search of breakfast.

He kicked the smoldering ends onto the bed of live coals and added a few sticks. Into a tin of hot water he dumped a couple of handfuls of coffee, and packed up while it simmered over the red embers.

Across his mind ambled the thought that Whitley might get to Roan before he did and spook him into running. That could cost him time tracking Roan down, and delay his getting back to Junction City in time to pay Hogan.

He was determined not to give Hogan that satisfaction. He gulped his coffee, kicked out the fire, and climbed into the saddle. The bulge under his shirt on the left side told him the bag of gold was safe. He spurred the mare into an easy canter, and set out on the last leg of his ride to Buffalo Flats.

Nine

The mare picked her way up the draw toward a stand of cottonwoods.

Savage reflected on the six days he had sweated over the wind-swept prairie of western Kansas. He had fought the tedium of gray-green sedge grass, and the monotony broken only by the chatter of chipmunks, yipping coyotes, and the blood-curdling threat of a restless rattler.

In the saddle by day, feet to the fire by night, most of his life he had battled heat, cold, and rain. But through it all, his worst enemy was the loneliness that rode with him wherever he went. And now, the sweat of his horse, and the pungent odor of his own unwashed body, made him eager for a hot bath and a shave, and a good meal cooked in somebody's kitchen.

His body told him he needed to spend some time in a good woman's bed, reminding him of when he had first met Meg McGraff.

Savage had been on the trail of Mac Corliss west of Great Bend. Corliss was a cattle rustler and brand switcher who had eluded the law for three years. Savage spotted him by a campfire at sundown. Corliss went for his gun, and Savage shot him dead. He hauled his body into town and turned it over to Sheriff Webb.

Webb checked the body draped over the saddle of Corliss's black horse.

"You finally got close enough to old Mac to do him in, did you?" he said to Savage.

Savage nodded.

"Had to kill him, did you?" Webb said.

"He didn't want to come."

"Old Mac always was a stubborn bastard. Well, Savage," the sheriff said, leading the black away, "I'll take charge of this old boy. If you run into Ben Cassidy, tell him Spider Webb said howdy."

"I will."

Darkness was closing in. Savage was tired and hungry, and needed a place to bed down for the night, before the ride back to Abilene. Across the street from the sheriff's office was the Devil's Hole Saloon. Savage headed that way.

Behind the bar was a redheaded young woman with a smile about three hands wide.

"What's the matter, cowboy?" she said. "You look like you just lost your last friend."

"I must be tireder than I thought," Savage said.

"How about a shot of tiger juice? That'll bring you back to life."

She placed a glass on the bar and poured it full of whiskey.

Savage sipped at it.

"Is there some place around here where a man could get some supper?" he said.

The redhead gave him a sideways look.

"How hungry are you?" she said.

"Hungry as a coyote that last ate a week ago Tuesday."

"That's you, huh?"

"That's me."

She liked this man. He was forthright and easygoing. Not like the rowdies who blew in, got drunk, and caused trouble.

And he was hungry.

"Can you wait a few minutes?" she said.

"Well, I don't plan on starving for about another half hour."

She refilled his glass and leaned across the bar.

"The best supper in town is at my place," she said. "As soon as Slim shows up to spell me, I'll cook it for you."

She was as good as her word. She placed before him an inch-thick steak with mashed potatoes and gravy, topped off with a huge serving of fresh peach cobbler.

"I bet you like your coffee hot and black," she said.

"I do."

She poured two cups full, then sat down across from him, sipped her coffee, and watched him eat.

"My name is Meg McGraff," she said. "I've lived for twenty-eight years, and I've known a lot of men, but looking at you, watching you eat, listening to you talk— Well, you stir stuff in me that I forgot I had."

Savage nodded, and tipped his coffee cup.

"Will Savage," he said.

Meg lifted her cup in his direction.

"You have no idea how long it has been since I saw a grown man blush," she said.

"Well, I—"

"You'll need a place to put up for the night," Meg had said. "If you're like me, you don't like sleeping alone."

Savage dwelt on the memory until the mare reached the mouth of the draw. She nickered softly, and perked her ears forward, telling Savage something was taking place up ahead.

"Throw a rope over that big limb." Savage heard a whiskey-hoarse voice say. "Let's get this horse thiever hung 'fore dark."

"Hold it, Luke," Savage heard another man say. "Rider coming up the draw."

Savage saw a husky man in a black hat and faded Levi's astride a bay gelding. The mare came up out of the draw, and Savage reined her to at the edge of a clearing.

With a squint-eyed curiosity, the man called Luke said, "Howdy, stranger."

"Howdy," Savage said.

"You lost?" Half smiling, ruddy-faced.

"Nope."

"Whatcha doing here then?"

"Passing by."

"All right," Luke said. He pushed his dirty black Stetson to the back of his head. "Keep on a-passing."

Savage eyed the man on each side of Luke. The one on his right was skinny, red-faced, and fair-haired. On Luke's left was a chunky older man, maybe forty-five, graying at the temples, a twitch to his mouth. Savage thought they both looked scared.

In his left hand Luke held the loose end of a lariat. Savage followed it with his eyes to the other end, where a noose was looped around the neck of a young boy. The boy was standing on the ground, hands tied behind him, with a terrified look on his face.

"Having a party?" Savage said.

Luke said, "Who the hell wants to know?"

"I the hell do." Savage spat a streak of tobacco juice. "Wondering why you've got a rope around that boy's neck."

"Horse-thievin'. He rode my horse right off from in front of the Last Dog Saloon. Frank here seen him do it."

"Uh-huh."

Savage took another look at the boy, trying to satisfy himself as to what was going on. He spat another streak of tobacco juice while he thought about it, and watched it form little craters in the dust. He wiped his mouth on the back of his hand.

"I guess the marshal knows about this, does he?" he said.

"Castledine?" Luke said. He and his friends shared a brief laugh about that. "That whoring bastard?"

Savage made a mental note of the marshal's name.

"Whose horse are you riding now?" he said.

"Mine," Luke said.

"How did you get him back?"

"Mister, you sure ask a lot of questions."

"How did you get your horse back?" Savage said.

"Found him tied in front of the Last Dog."

The fidgety man on Luke's left said, "Let's get this over with, Luke"

"Just hold on, Curly," Luke said. "I'll handle this."

Savage said, "How come you're in such an all-fired sweat to get that boy hung?"

Luke had the answer. "Ain't fittin' for a man to hang overnight."

"That's not a man you're hanging."

"Horse-thievin' is horse-thievin'," Luke said. "They all look the same to me."

"Did you ask him why he took your horse?"

"Hell no. If he steals a horse, he'll lie about why."

"Come on, Luke," said the man on Luke's left.

"Shut up, Frank!"

To the boy, Savage said, "How old are you, son?"

"Twelve, sir."

"Did you ever steal a horse before?"

"No, sir. I just took it to get my mama some medicine. She was bad sick."

"See there, Luke," Savage said. "It wasn't really stealing. The boy never meant to keep your horse. Why don't you let him go?"

"Let him go?" Luke cast a nervous glance at Curly and Frank.

"You got your horse back. He won't take it again."

"I aim to make sure of that."

Savage made a quick judgment of Frank and Curly. They weren't spoiling for a fight, but they would follow Luke's lead if it came to that.

To Luke, he said, "Why don't you tell old Curly to move over there and cut the boy loose?"

Luke was itching to make a play against this nosy stranger who had interrupted his lynching party, but he wasn't sure of his chances. With a look, he sought support from Curly and Frank, but didn't get it.

Savage figured that would give him an edge in a ruckus.

"You talk mighty big for a man facing three," Luke said.

Savage spat, wiped his mouth, and studied Luke's sweating brow. If he thought he could beat Savage to the draw, he'd have tried before now.

"Who the hell are you anyhow?" Luke said.

"Just somebody waiting to see who'll get the rope off that boy's neck."

"Luke!"

"Hold on. Curly."

"I'm counting to ten," Savage said, "and I'm already up to five."

"Luke!"

"Shut up, Frank!"

In a single motion, as though they had held a meeting to decide what to do, Frank and Curly reined their mounts backward out of the clearing, jerked them around, and took off at a dead run.

"Frank! Curly!" Luke yelled. "Come back here, you—"

"Time's up, Luke," Savage said. "What'll it be?"

Luke said, "All right. Let him go."

"You tied him up. You let him go."

The two glared at each other. Luke hadn't given up on making a play.

Savage expected him to try, but uncertainty hobbled the bully's hand.

Slowly he moved toward the boy. He kept a wary eye on Savage while he removed the noose from the boy's neck, then untied his hands.

Tearful and shaken, the boy breathed a deep sigh and rubbed his wrists where the rope left red marks on his skin.

Luke cast Savage a vengeful look, then spurred his bay out of the clearing.

He then spun around, ripped out his gun, and slung a shot at Savage.

Savage had anticipated the move and buried a slug in Luke's chest. Luke tumbled off his horse and fell to the ground in a heap.

"Stand away, son," Savage said to the boy.

Savage held his gun on the fallen roughneck, while he dismounted, then toed Luke's lifeless body over face up.

"He ain't moving, mister," the boy said

"Do you know who this man is, son?"

"Yes, sir. He's Luke Barefoot."

"There was no call for this."

"No, sir."

"Bull-headedness kills more men than guns. Well, we'll put him on his horse, and you can ride up with me."

They draped Luke's body over the bay. Savage then climbed into the saddle, and handed the boy up behind him.

"What's your name, boy?" Savage said, gigging the mare out of the clearing.

"Henry Wadsworth."

"Is that so? The only Henry Wadsworth I ever heard of was a poem writer. Long, dull stuff that folks had a time wading through." He shot a streak of tobacco juice into the dust. "Are you a poem writer, Henry?"

At ease now, the boy giggled.

"No, sir," he said.

"Do you go to school?"

"Yes, sir, in Buffalo Flats."

"You live in Buffalo Flats?"

"Yes, sir. Me and my mama."

"We better get you home. Late as it is, your mama's likely worried sick about you."

"Yep, that's how Mama is."

"Is your daddy in Buffalo Flats too?"

"Reckon I never had one."

Savage gave the boy a serious look and wondered what had become of his father.

They fell silent. Savage spat and wiped his chin, his mind on Luke Barefoot.

He guessed it was easier for some men to die than to live.

Up ahead he caught sight of a figure outlined against the setting sun.

"Somebody coming," he said.

He heard an anxious voice call, "Henry!"

"That's my mama," Henry said. "You better get shut of that chaw."

"How's that?"

"Mama don't cotton to chawin' or dippin' or smokin'."

Savage spat the juicy glob onto the prairie sod.

Henry slid off the mare's rump and ran to meet his mother. Small of stature, dark hair knotted in the back, Mrs. Wadsworth was dressed in an ankle length skirt and a long-sleeved white blouse. Savage guessed her to be about thirty-five.

She grabbed her son and clutched him to her.

"Oh, Henry!" she cried. "They told me those awful men carried you away. I was afraid I'd never see you again!"

Henry clung to her waist.

"Don't cry, Mama," he said.

"How could they do such a horrible thing? Just a boy, and they—"

Her eyes found the tall cowboy sitting the sorrel mare.

Savage watched her with an amused smile.

"Howdy, ma'am," he said, touching the brim of his hat. "I'm Will Savage."

"Oh!" she gasped with a hand to her mouth. "Who is that?"

Henry said, "That's Luke Barefoot, mama."

"Is he—uh—"

"I'm pretty sure he is, ma'am," Savage said. "He hasn't moved for a while."

"How did he—uh—"

"I shot him."

"You shot—" She gasped again, almost choking on the words. "You killed this man, and you just sit there like—like—"

"Luke was one of them, mama," Henry said. "Mr. Savage made him take the noose off my neck."

"How awful!" To Savage, she said, "You could have been killed!"

"You should have seen him, Mama," Henry burst in. "Three of them, there was, and Mr. Savage—he stared 'em down! Two of 'em took off like scared rabbits, and this one here, old Luke, got hisself killed 'cause he fired at Mr. Savage. Then wham! Bam! Mr. Savage fired back, and old Luke, he just fell right off that big old horse and died!"

"Savage?" Mrs. Wadsworth said, brow wrinkled, trying to remember.

"Will Savage?"

"You got me red-handed, ma'am."

"They say you were a gunman, a hired killer for the Cattleman's Association."

"Well, now you're wrong about that, ma'am." He threw a leg over the mare's rump and stood down. "Some folks are good at farming, some sell calico in a store. I was always pretty good with a gun. That's the only kind of good some people understand."

Mrs. Wadsworth surveyed the trail-dusty cowboy with a curious eye. He was taller than he had appeared in the saddle.

"Perhaps," she said.

Savage turned away.

"Mr. Savage," she said. "I'm Sarah Wadsworth. I appreciate what you did for my son today. Would you stay to supper?"

Savage climbed into the saddle.

"That's mighty kind of you, ma'am, but I have to report this to the marshal."

"Later perhaps?"

Savage glanced at Henry, and put a spur to the mare, "Perhaps," he said.

Ten

"**W**here is Castledine?"

For the answer a handful of men milling around in front of the General Mercantile looked to their leader, the chubby Mayor Claddock. The mayor, in his gray Chesterfield and black derby, was at a loss to explain the whereabouts of the town marshal.

"Who knows?" said he. "Probably off humping some whore!"

"Hold it," someone said. "Here he comes now."

The group fell silent and watched the leisurely approach of a shiny black stallion with the imposing figure of Marshal John Castledine in the saddle.

The marshal was in no hurry. Coal black hair that matched his clipped mustache brushed his shoulders. His piercing black eyes scanned the huddle of cronies as he pulled up. In a calm, authoritative baritone, he asked what the commotion was about.

The mayor assumed his position as spokesman, and said, "Somebody said they saw Will Savage out by the Widow Wadsworth's place."

Castledine cast him a puzzled look.

"Savage?" he said.

A hawk-faced man in a crumpled brown hat said, "He shot Luke Barefoot."

Castledine said, "Who is Will Savage?"

The mayor squeaked, "You mean you don't know who Will Savage is?"

"I'm afraid not."

"Well," a crabby voice said, "what're you gonna do about it?"

With a dubious eye the marshal surveyed the irascible faces challenging him to "do something" about a man he didn't know, had never seen nor heard of. He knew this bunch had worked themselves into a tizzy before over something that didn't amount to a scoop of horse apples. If this man Savage showed up in Buffalo Flats, then he would have to decide what to do about him. Meanwhile, the marshal had no time to waste on a gaggle of babblers.

He did, however, make a decision.

"Right now," he said, "I'm going to have a good hot bath and a good hot supper."

"And maybe a good hot woman!" the mayor jeered.

Castledine ignored him, and gigged the black toward Mrs. McClellan's Boarding House down the street. "If this Savage fellow shows up, tell him I'll be in my office in an hour."

"Hell of a marshal!" someone shouted at his departing back. "The whole town's about to get blowed up, and the marshal goes a-whorin'!

Eleven

Savage dismounted and dropped a rein over the hitch rail in front of the Last Dog Saloon.

The mayor and his hangers-on eyed him with suspicion.

Savage nodded toward the body draped over the bay.

"Anybody know this man?" he said.

The hawk-faced man grabbed a handful of the dead man's hair and lifted the goggle-eyed head.

"That's old Luke all right," he said.

Savage asked if anyone had seen the marshal.

That triggered a scornful twitter that made its way around the circle.

"He said he'd be in his office in an hour," the mayor sneered, "but I wouldn't count on it if I was you."

"And who are you, sir?" Savage said.

"Why, I'm the mayor of this fair city, and if you, sir, are who I believe you to be, your reputation has preceded you here. You would do well to watch your step, or you could find yourself in a heap of trouble."

Savage offered him a sardonic smile.

"I'll try to remember that," he said. To the man in the brown hat, he said, "How long ago was the marshal here?"

"Thirty minutes outside."

"Would you take care of Mr. Barefoot for me? I'm going in here and have a beer while I wait for the marshal."

The man led the bay away to Hezzy Thorne's funeral parlor down the street, and Savage mounted the steps to the Last Dog Saloon.

The Last Dog hadn't changed much in the four years since he last saw it. Rough-hewn log walls, the bar stretching along the left side, a half dozen tables and chairs scattered about. Some of the tables were surrounded by poker-faced card players. Slouching at the bar, three punchers traded stories.

Nothing different—except for the steps leading up from the far side of the room. Charlie must have added some rooms up there.

"Beer," Savage said to the fat young bartender with a broad smile. "Does Charlie Crum still own this place?"

"Yep, Charlie still owns it," the man said, pouring a glass full of beer.

"Is he around?"

"Not tonight. He's not back from Dodge yet."

Savage heard a stir to his right.

A hush fell over the room. Play at the tables stopped. Wary cowpokes, smelling the makings of a gunfight, scurried to line up against the wall to watch, or scampered out the door to escape flying lead.

In the back-bar mirror Savage caught the image of a stocky man with a three-inch knife scar down his left cheek. The man was staring at him from the end of the bar to Savage's right. The starer wore a brace of pearl handled revolvers. He was flanked by two hombres Savage had seen before. Frank and Curly, the ones who ran out on Luke.

Savage shifted the beer to his left hand. Keeping an eye on the scar-faced one in the mirror, he concentrated on his drink.

"That's him there," he heard a husky voice say.

"Are you Savage?" said the scar-faced image in the mirror.

Savage nodded to the mirror. "I'm Savage."

In a flat, toneless voice, the man said, "I'm Wilson Barefoot."

If Barefoot expected Savage to be shocked, he was disappointed. The presence of Frank and Curly took the edge off what otherwise might have been a surprise.

Savage lifted his glass to the mirror in a casual salute.

"I don't like it when people don't look at me when I talk to them," Barefoot said.

Savage took a brief look. He saw the angry redness working its way into Barefoot's cheeks. He figured this one had more grit than his brother. Curly and Frank, standing stiff as wagon tongues, appeared no more anxious for a fight than before.

Savage sipped at his beer.

"What else don't you like, Mr. Barefoot?" he said.

"I don't like people killing my brother."

"Is that the one I brought in on the bay?"

"You know damn well—"

"Your brother was a fool, Barefoot. There's no call for you to be the same." With a nod, he said, "Howdy, Frank. Curly."

The two henchmen shifted uneasily from one foot to the other, waiting for a sign from Barefoot.

"My brother was hanging a horse thief," Barefoot said.

"Your brother was hanging a twelve-year-old boy who brought the horse back to where he got it. It was all over. All Luke had to do was ride out. He decided not to." With a tinge of sarcasm, he said, "You talked to Frank and Curly. I'm sure they told you the straight of it."

"I aim to kill you, Savage."

"Uh-huh," Savage grunted. "You gonna do it, or stand around all night talking about it?"

Four guns cleared leather. Savage leaped to his right. Firing in the same motion, he took cover behind an overturned table. He saw Barefoot's body plop to the floor beside the bar. He saw the bodies of Frank and Curly plop on top of Barefoot. And when the smoke cleared, he saw a stubby little red bearded man crouching near the batwing doors, leveling his smoking gun at where Frank and Curly had stood seconds before.

Amos Cully grinned at him.

"I told you I could be a heap of help to you," Cully said.

Savage nodded, holstered his gun, and pumped the little man's hand.

"Thanks," he said, "till you're better paid."

Savage checked the bulge under his shirt on the left side. The bag of gold was safely in place. He wondered how long he would be safe carrying it around.

With Cully at his side, he headed for the door in search of Marshal John Castledine.

Twelve

Savage and Cully brushed past the huddle of mollycoddles and mounted their horses.

To no one in particular, Savage said, "Tell the marshal I'll see him later."

"You'll see the marshal now."

Savage turned to his left and looked into the face of a big man dressed in black, mounted on a black stallion. On his chest was pinned a silver star.

Savage motioned Cully to go ahead. "Maybe I'll run into you later," he said.

Reining the mare about, Savage fell in beside the marshal. At the jail they dismounted, and Castledine led the way in. He tossed his black Stetson at a wooden peg on the wall, and motioned Savage to a chair across from his desk. Savage stood.

"You've been busy," the marshal said. "Do you want to tell me about it? Or, based on what I've heard, would you rather I just threw your ass in jail and kept you there until the judge decides to come around, maybe sometime next year?"

"Well, I don't know what you've heard—"

"Let me tell you what I've heard." Castledine leaned forward, eyes flashing. "I've heard you shot and killed Luke Barefoot. And now there are three more men dead because you egged them into a fight."

"That's not quite accurate."

"I run a clean town here, Savage. There hasn't been a killing in Buffalo Flats since I got here two years ago. You've been around for a couple of hours and already four men are dead because of you."

"Now, hold on there, marshal."

"The way I get it, you stopped Luke Barefoot from hanging a horse thief."

"He was hanging a twelve-year-old boy."

"What? A boy?"

"The boy said he borrowed the horse to get his mama medicine for some kind of sickness."

"Who was the boy?"

"Henry Wadsworth."

"Henry?" The marshal showed some interest. "The Widow Wadsworth's boy?"

"That's right. They had the noose around his neck."

"What happened out there?"

"Like I told his brother, all Luke had to do was ride out, but he drew down on me, and I shot him."

From his vest pocket, the marshal drew a heavy silver watch. He glanced at it, then dropped it back into the pocket.

"What about Wilson Barefoot?" Castledine said.

"I brought Luke's body in on his horse. While I was waiting for you, I had a beer. Wilson Barefoot showed up with the same two yahoos that were with Luke, Curly and Frank."

"And what happened then?"

"Barefoot said he aimed to kill me. That's when the fireworks started."

"Who's the man you called Amos?"

"Amos Cully, a friend from Abilene."

"All right. It looks like you were in the right. But I'll be checking you out before I decide for sure."

"Check away," Savage said. "I do seem to draw attention at times. Shots get fired, and you never know when one of them might hit somebody."

"You better walk with a light step around here, Savage. I don't want to be locking you up, but I will if it comes to that."

Savage bristled. "If there's trouble, it'll be somebody else's doing. I came here looking for a man, not trouble."

"A man? Who?"

Again Castledine checked his watch.

Savage figured the marshal was more anxious to get some place else than to hear what he had to say.

"It'll keep," he said. "After I find him I'll be gone, then you can go to hell and take your town with you. And, marshal—" He pinned him with a steady gaze. "Any man I ever shot needed shooting."

"Were you the judge of that?"

"Me and him."

"How's that?"

"He decided."

Savage made a move toward the door.

"One more thing, Savage."

Savage waited.

"There's a whole pot full of those Barefooots out there, in Nebraska and Oklahoma Territory. What you've done could lead to a young war. If it comes to that, I will throw your ass in jail."

Savage slammed the door behind him as he left.

Thirteen

Cully was dug in at a poker table in the far corner of the Last Dog Saloon, dealing a hand around the table. Four other men tossed their antes into the pot.

Savage squatted beside Amos's chair.

"Howdy, podnah," Amos said. "You get off the hook with the marshal?"

"So far. I think he wishes I was some place else. Are you gonna be here all night?"

"I sure might be. I'm up a passel. I don't think these fellers would take kindly to me takin' off with their money."

"I'll be out to the Widow Wadsworth's."

Amos's wry grin was not lost on Savage.

"Well now, she asked me to supper and I think I ought to go."

"I think you're plum right. Be damned if I wouldn't do the same in your place. Raise five," he said, sweetening the pot. "If you don't show up here by morning, what'll I tell the folks back home?"

"Tell them I was hung for strangling a dirty-minded friend with a red beard."

Cully chortled, and Savage left.

Fourteen

John Castledine rapped on the door to Room 203.

A soft voice from the other side said, "Is that you, John?"

"It's me."

"Come on in."

Castledine turned the knob, and eased open the door. He stepped into the room, then closed the door behind him.

"You're late," said the blond woman with hazel eyes. She was sitting in the middle of her bed, dealing solitaire. Stark naked.

"Hello, Carrie."

Fifteen

Sarah Wadsworth's modest frame home was encircled by a white picket fence. Savage dropped a rein over the gatepost. The gate opened to a narrow stone path leading to the front door splashed with the glow of a high yellow moon.

"I'm glad you decided to accept my invitation," Sarah said from the porch swing, as though she'd been expecting him "After the way I acted earlier, I wouldn't have blamed you if you never wanted to see me again."

One look told Savage this was not the same Sarah Wadsworth he had met earlier. Her manner was relaxed, her smile warm. Her dark hair fell loosely about her narrow shoulders. Savage thought she looked younger than the thirty-five years he'd guessed her to be.

"I waited supper for you," she said, as he stepped onto the porch.

"That's real nice of you, ma'am. When a man gets to be as old as I am, some habits are hard to break."

"How old are you?"

"Thirty-seven."

"That's pretty old," she said with a wry smile, and led the way inside.

"And what habits can't you break?"

"One of them is eating. I haven't had a good home-cooked meal for so long my stomach has been doing cartwheels just thinking about it."

From the wood-burning stove she brought a pan of hot water, poured the water into a basin, and invited Savage to wash up.

She then pulled out the cane-bottom chair at the head of the table, and he sat on it.

"I hoped you would come," she said. "I fixed what I thought you'd like."

On the table she set a plate of fluffy biscuits, a platter of golden fried chicken, and green beans fresh from her garden.

She sat across the table. "I want to thank you again for what you did for my son today."

"Yes, ma'am."

She passed him the chicken platter.

"Can I make a bargain with you?" she said.

"I reckon."

"If you'll stop calling me ma'am, and start calling me Sarah, I might invite you to supper again sometime."

Savage reddened, nodded. "Where's Henry?" he said. "Did he have supper?"

"Henry had supper. It's a bit past his bedtime."

Savage felt her eyes on him, and concentrated on his food.

She passed the biscuits, their eyes met, and he looked away.

"Henry tells me you haven't been well," he said.

"Not well?" She seemed surprised. "I'm all right. I have little dizzy spells sometimes, but I'm all right."

"Uh-huh. What does the doctor say?"

"The only doctor around here is twenty-seven miles away in Dodge City. Old Doc Stark comes around about every month or so, but he doesn't have time for dizzy spells."

She brought the coffee pot and poured their cups full.

"That's why we're here in Buffalo Flats. We came from St. Louis where Henry was born. One day the doctor told me I needed clean, fresh air. So, we moved out here. A year later my husband was killed in a stage holdup. I became the village seamstress and washer woman, so Henry and I could stay here."

She refilled his cup.

"I hear there was some trouble between you and Wilson Barefoot," she said, avoiding his eyes. "You told me you weren't a gunslinger."

"I believe what I said was that I never killed for money."

"Have you killed many?"

He brushed his chin with a white cloth napkin, and tried to find a way to answer her question, wondering why he wanted to.

"I've killed some," he said.

"Some?"

"Several."

"A lot?"

"How many is a lot, Sarah?"

Savage thought she was pretty worked up about it, but he felt no obligation to hold school on the ethics of gun fighting. He decided it was time to go. He stood up and reached for his hat.

"Will you be long in Buffalo Flats?" Sarah said.

"A few days. Maybe a week. It depends."

"On what?"

There was no need to keep it a secret. Sarah might know something that would help him locate Roan.

"A judge in Abilene asked me to deliver a reward to a man named Aubrey Roan. Roan was last known to be headed this way."

"What did this Roan fellow do to deserve the reward?"

Savage didn't feel the need to go into all the details, but he had come this far.

"He killed a man in Abilene."

"Roan is an outlaw then?"

"Yes. But there was a reward for the man he killed. I mention it only because I thought you might have seen or heard something that would help me find him."

52

"The only thing I've— Well, there was a man by here who asked for a drink of water, and I gave it to him." She paused for a moment, then said, "I thought it strange that he asked the name of the town marshal in Buffalo Flats."

"That's Castledine?"

"Yes. John Castledine."

"Did you get the man's name?"

"No. He was here for only a minute. He thanked me for the water, and rode away on a big roan horse."

"How long ago was that?"

"Well, out here we tend to lose track of time, you know. I'd say maybe a week or so ago."

Savage gave his head a thoughtful nod.

"Oh," she said. "There was one other thing. His eyes. They were never still, always looking over his shoulder. Like he was expecting somebody to come up behind him."

Savage gave his head a thoughtful nod.

"Thank you, Sarah." He pressed his hat on, and said, "Thank you for supper. I'll be going now."

Sarah wasn't ready for him to leave.

"Could I tempt you with a piece of my fresh apple pie and one more cup of coffee?"

Savage was anxious to be gone, but he couldn't resist her smiling invitation. He dropped his hat onto a chair.

He watched Sarah fill their coffee cups and serve the pie. In that floor length skirt he couldn't tell if she had legs, but he liked her full lips, and her pointed breasts that stuck out—like Carrie's used to.

Carrie. He sneaked away for a brief recollection, wishing he had spent more time at home with her. She never understood that his time away was to make sure their son—when they had one—would have a better life than he could offer at the time.

Sarah's voice brought him back.

"I'm glad you came to supper," she said. "I hope you'll find the time to come again."

"I will."

Sixteen

Breakfast came early at Mrs. McClellan's Boarding House. Cully didn't show up until almost seven. The tables were spread with red-and- white checkered cloths. He spotted Savage at one of them, and headed that way.

Half a dozen other men, including a couple of drummers and Marshal John Castledine, were busy with food and conversation over coffee.

Amos threw a leg over the back of a chair and sat down across from Savage.

"Well, it looks like I won't be takin' no sad messages back to the home folks," he said. He waved at Sally Tole, and she came for his order.

"Two fried eggs—drop 'em in and take 'em out—biscuits and sausage."

Castledine passed their table on his way out, and traded nods with Savage.

Amos said, "I bet you're not one of the marshal's favorite people."

"He said there hadn't been a killing in Buffalo Flats for two years, and didn't appreciate having four in one day." With a steady look, he said, "If it hadn't been for you, I might have been one of them."

Cully studied the bottom of his coffee cup like he was trying to see through it, stirring in cream and sugar.

"How come you're not still back there in that saloon in Abilene where I left you?" Savage said. "Why did you ride all the way out here anyhow?"

Amos raked a sleeve across his mouth.

"I follered you," he said with a sheepish grin. "Back in Abilene I heard a couple fellers talkin' like they was gonna jump you before you got here. I didn't want nothin' happenin' to you, 'cause you'd think I done it, and I never would."

With an appreciative nod, Savage said, "Did you run into any trouble?"

"I skeered off a couple of yahoos that I thought might cause some."

Considering how many people knew about the bag of gold, Savage had thought it strange that on his ride from Abilene to Buffalo Flats nobody tried to take it away from him. Now he knew why.

"They was this one feller name of Whitley," Amos said. "Said he needed to ketch up to you. He looked too old to cause much trouble, so I didn't slow him down."

"He found me. He wanted me to get Roan for him. Something about a Lawman's Protective Association."

Amos nodded. "What about Roan, Will?"

"Keep it under your hat for now. Reward or not, if Roan gets wind that we're here about Freeman, he's likely to run, and I can't afford the time it would take to hunt him down."

"Be damned if I wouldn't in his place! If somebody was on my tail for somethin' I done, I'd make myself scarcer than a dominacker rooster at a Sunday school chicken fry. I mean, I'd find myself a holler log and hole up in it till the Lord come again."

Savage pushed away from the table and stood up.

"A friend of mine used to live out west about three miles," he said. "He knew everything that went on around here. I'm going to take a ride out and see if he's still there." On his way out, he said, "Keep your eyes and ears peeled, Amos. You never know when you might run across something."

"I will. Say, Will."

"Yeah?"

"How'd you and that widow woman get along last night?"

"She's a fine lady, Amos. A real fine lady."

Amos grinned and watched him go. "Ask me no questions," he muttered to himself, "and I'll tell you no lies." He waved at Sally to bring more coffee.

Seventeen

A thin wisp of gray smoke wafted lazily out the chimney pipe sticking through the roof of the weather beaten shanty hunkered on the west bank of Little Turkey Creek. Savage thought that was a good sign that Cap'n Billy Beauchamp was still there. Who else, he asked himself with a grin, would spend the rest of his life in such a rundown shanty?

The pungent odor of burning firewood attacked his nostrils as he forded the stream below a stand of cottonwoods. Approaching the cabin, he was greeted by an assortment of panting, wet-tongued mongrels. Cap'n Billy believed the only thing better than being alone was being surrounded by a passel of barking, leaping dogs.

From inside the shack, Savage heard a husky voice he recognized as that of Cap'n Billy Beauchamp. The dogs got quiet, but continued romping about as though it had been a while since they had company.

Savage dismounted and waded through the dogs to the cabin door.

"Cap'n Billy, " he called. "Oh, Cap'n Billy."

He heard a stir to his right, and the dogs bounded that way. Savage saw the muzzle of a double-barreled shotgun jutting out from around the corner of the house.

"Hold it right there, mister!" Billy growled. He leveled the gun at Savage's belt buckle. "Don't make a move or I'll kill you." He spat a stream of tobacco juice. "What're you sneakin' around here for anyhow?" Again he spat, squinting for a closer look.

Cap'n Billy was a grizzled old codger with a scraggly yellowing mustache and a heavy beard that hadn't seen scissors nor razor for longer than he could remember. In the summer of 1876 he'd served as an army scout for General George Armstrong Custer at the battle of Little Big Horn. He had tried to convince Custer not to attack the five thousand Indians ranged against him, but Custer was hell-bent to conquer the Sioux with a force of only 268 cavalry. They all died along with Custer in the bloody battle. Cap'n Billy lived to tell about it only because he was sent back for reinforcements.

He had also spent time hunting buffalo, trapping beaver, and fighting mountain lions. Living the life of a hermit, he was content to make a home for the dozen or so mongrels he called "my boys." He asked no more of the world than that it leave him alone.

Savage kept an eye on the shotgun, hoping to convince the old timer not to use it on him.

"I'm Will Savage, Cap'n Billy."

"You ain't no Will Savage! Will Savage is dead, rest his soul. State your business and git out, or I'll turn them dogs loose, and they'll turn your vitals into vittles 'fore you can holler git."

"Let me step a little closer, so you can see my face."

"Ain't nothin' wrong with my seein'! I knowed Will Savage half his life. I 'bout keeled over myself when I heard he died in that Injun raid."

Savage eased a couple of steps toward him until the sunlight fell full on his face.

Cap'n Billy squinted again, and took a longer look.

"Savage?" he said, confused. He took a cautious step forward. "Is that really you, Will?"

"It's me, Cap'n Billy."

The old warrior leaned the shotgun against the wall of the shack. With a broad grin, he opened his arms, and welcomed Savage with a bear hug.

"Will Savage!" he said, leading the way inside. "Come on in this house. I was just stirrin' up some grub for my boys. They git grumpy if they don't eat reg'lar. You et, Will?"

"I had breakfast in town. Thanks anyway."

Built into the corner of the shack was a bed frame of sycamore limbs. On the frame lay a thin mattress with the stuffing bulging out at the seams.

On top of the pot-bellied stove in the middle of the dirt floor, steam wafted from a rusty syrup bucket filled with leaves, dried grass, and chunks of 'possum fat. The aroma of brewed coffee rose from a blackened pot next to the stew bucket.

Billy brought out two stained tin cups and poured them full of coffee. He handed one to Savage, and lifted the other to his lips.

"Welcome home, Will," he said with a wide grin. "I figgered I'd never see you again."

Savage sipped at his coffee while he brought Billy up-to-date on what had happened to him since they last met. He included the episode with Denver Dunn, and how he had been picked up by the cavalry patrol.

Billy had heard about that, but he listened, studying his friend's face, and gave him an affectionate slap on the shoulder. He knew Savage didn't ride all the way out there to tell him his life story.

"I seen that look afore, Will," he said. "That look in your eye. Restless as a hound dog at a rabbit hole. Like they's somethin' you can't wait to get said."

"Well, Cap'n Billy, you're right. I'm looking for a man."

"I shoulda seen that coming."

"His name is Aubrey Roan. I thought you might know something about him. I hear he has been seen around here lately."

"I might. Sometimes a feller will ride by and tell me things he don't think I'll recollect nohow." He aimed a streak of tobacco juice at the ashcan by the stove. "It ain't been more'n a week or two since some young buck come aridin' by here. I challenged him with my equalizer, like I did you, Will. The feller says he's lookin' for some place to put up for a few days till he can git settled. I'm thinkin', why don't he put up at the boardin' house in town, but I never said nothin'.about it."

"Roan is about thirty years old, sandy hair, stocky build."

"Well, it's been so dad-blamed long since I seen thirty I wouldn't reco'nize it if it hit me in the face, but I'd cal'clate this old boy was nigh onto thirty.

"I never felt plum good 'bout havin' him around. But, he acted kinda lost, so I took him in. He was around here for two or three days, first and last. Then one day I went coyote shootin', and when I got back he was gone. I ain't seen hide nor hair of him since."

"Did he tell you his name?"

Cap'n Billy shook his woolly head. "He never told me, and I never asked. But they was somethin' mighty pecooler 'bout that old boy, Will."

"What's that?"

"His eyes. They was all the time a-movin'. Like he was lookin' for somebody or 'nother."

Sarah Wadsworth had told him the same thing.

"Stranger'n a goose at a gander rally," Billy said. "And that big old horse o' his— Never seen a horse that big in all my put-togethers."

"A roan, was it?"

Billy nodded. "Big old roan stallion. Biggest horse ever I seen."

Savage was anxious to get away. He was convinced that the man Cap'n Billy described, backed up by what he'd heard from Sarah, was Aubrey Roan.

Savage guessed that Roan, thinking his trail had grown cold, was in no hurry to move on.

But he couldn't afford to count on that.

Eighteen

Any time he saw his little brother coming, John Castledine was stricken with an acute case of wanting to be some place else. Born to John's widowed mother after she married Cliff Roan, Aubrey carried the brand of trouble, and the marshal wasn't anxious to find out what kind he was dragging behind him this time.

Nor was Aubrey eager for him to find out.

Aubrey left Joe Freeman dead on the floor of Golly Moses's livery in Abilene and drifted to Great Bend, Wichita, and Colby. He hoped that time and distance would dim his trail, and that his killing the marshal would soon be forgotten.

But, he knew better. He knew somebody would be coming after him. He didn't know who, and he didn't know when. He knew his days of looking over his shoulder to see who was coming up behind him would not end until somebody did. And he needed a place to hide.

In Colby Aubrey had pistol whipped a man for besting him in a poker game. The Colby sheriff ran him out of town with a warning never to show up there again.

Roan struck out for Buffalo Flats, where he heard his brother was the marshal. He hadn't wanted to drift beyond the shadow of Castledine's badge in case he needed his help. But he was glad Castledine hadn't invited him to stay with him at

A Bag of Gold

Mrs. McClellan's Boarding House, because he knew his big brother would explode if he found out why he was hiding out.

The couple of days Aubrey spent with the old codger and his dogs gave him time to scout around for a place far enough from town that Castledine wouldn't be breathing down his neck with his big brother routine. In his wanderings, Roan found an abandoned line shack, half hidden by a stand of sycamores. "Ain't much," he conceded, "but it'll do."

Ambling toward the shack one day, Roan spotted a young woman watering her horse at a stream. As he approached, her horse was spooked and took off at a dead run across the open prairie. The woman couldn't control the mount, and struggled to stay aboard.

Roan gave chase. He overtook the runaway, grabbed the bridle and brought the skittish animal to a standstill.

"Oh!" the woman gasped. "How can I ever thank you?"

Looking beyond the fright in her flushed face, Roan's eyes were drawn to the pouting lips, her hazel eyes with flecks of gold, and the mass of long, honey-colored hair.

"Just thank you seems so inadequate, Mister—"

Roan was busy taking in the shapely figure in the tight-fitting Levi's and loose white blouse.

"Roan," he said.

She held out a soft hand and he took it.

"Carrie Dunn, Mister Roan," she said. "How can I possibly repay you for saving my life?"

He was in no hurry to release her sweet-scented hand.

"Must be some way," he said.

His hungry-eyed stare, like a dog nosing a bitch in heat, was not lost on Carrie Dunn. With a provocative smile, she said, "Maybe a cup of coffee and some sugar cookies?"

Slowly she withdrew her hand.

"Maybe," Roan said.

"You might want to come calling sometime. I'm in room 203 at the Last Dog Saloon."

Roan had trouble concealing his excitement. He hadn't wanted to show up in town more often than necessary to pick up a few provisions, but he couldn't say no to the invitation of this luscious lady.

"When?" he said.

"How about tomorrow—about ten in the morning?" She reined her mount about. "I should be out of bed by then."

"Don't be surprised if I don't show up," Roan said. He tried to appear calm, though his heart was leaping like a frog in a gunny sack. "I stay busy."

Carrie put a spur to her horse's flank. Over her shoulder, she called, "I'll expect you at ten, Mr. Roan."

Roan watched horse and rider disappear in the distance. Already his loins were aflame with the fire of anticipation of sweeping Carrie Dunn off her tiny feet. Whisking her away to her huge featherbed, smothering her with kisses, and reveling in romantic ecstasy, the likes of which he was certain she had never known.

Nineteen

John Castledine was striding down the middle of the street,
like he had something serious on his mind.

Savage saw him coming and waited for him on the steps of
the Last Dog Saloon.

Castledine pulled up beside him.

"I sent some wires out on you," the marshal said. "It looks
to me like folks start living longer once you leave town."

"Is that so?"

"I'm satisfied you were in the right against the Barefoots,
but you've got a reputation for shooting and bloodshed, and
you had better walk with a careful step in this town."

Savage felt the heat of anger rising in his face.

"I get paid for keeping the peace," Castledine said, "and
I'm damn good at it."

"Uh-huh," Savage grunted. "So was Joe Freeman."

"Joe Freeman?"

"The marshal in Abilene. He was shot and killed a while
back."

"I heard about that. Joe was a good man. Is that the man
you're looking for—Joe's killer?"

Savage nodded.

"The word is he's been seen around Buffalo Flats. The
way I get it, Freeman was in some kind of trouble out west

before he showed up in Abilene. There was a reward for Freeman, dead or alive."

"I can't believe that."

"I'm telling you what the judge told me." Savage bristled. "Whether you believe it or not won't change it."

"A reward for killing a lawman?"

"Looks like Freeman wasn't always a lawman," Savage said. "Was he a friend of yours?"

"I knew him. We worked together a time or two. You say the man who shot him is in Buffalo Flats?"

"Here or hereabouts. A man named Aubrey Roan."

Castledine had a time hiding the shock of hearing his brother's name.

"Roan?" he said. "Aubrey Roan?"

"That's right."

"And he's entitled to the reward?"

"A thousand dollars."

Castledine shook his head. "I haven't seen anything on him. If I hear anything I'll get back to you."

"Thanks."

Savage tugged at his left earlobe. He thought the marshal acted like he was in a sweat to be some place else.

Twenty

Roan thought ten o'clock took too long to get there. When it did, he bounded up the back stairs of the Last Dog Saloon. With raging pulse he pushed open the door at the top of the stairs, and dashed into the shadowy hallway, looking for room 203. His knock was answered by the charming lady whose tantalizing smile he remembered from the day before. She stepped aside, and Roan swept past her, intoxicated by the scent of her perfume.

Carrie was dressed in a flowing skirt and snug-fitting blouse. Her honey colored hair brushed her narrow shoulders, and her hazel eyes were aglow.

She was even more ravishing than Roan remembered.

He couldn't get the door closed fast enough.

Carrie greeted him with a smile and a fresh cup of coffee. She needed Roan, but she also needed some time to devise her plan. She had detected Roan's devious nature from the beginning. Otherwise, she wouldn't have invited him to savor her sugar cookies. His weak eyes and lascivious leer told her he could be persuaded to get rid of Denver Dunn.

She never loved the slothful Dunn. Yet, convinced that Will had died in the Sioux raid, she had accepted Dunn's offer of marriage because she had no place else to turn. She learned early what a dolt he was, but stayed with him because of the baby son who arrived their first year together. Now, since she had become involved with the town marshal, Dunn was a millstone around her neck.

Woefully she led Roan to believe that she and Dunn were "not doing well together," but she must remain faithful to him because she promised "for better or worse." Still, she had sent her young son back east to live with relatives because she could no longer "bear the pain of seeing him abused by his tyrannical father." With tear-dimmed eyes she described the wretchedness of being separated from the boy.

Aubrey, in his frothing lust to crush to his boorish bosom the captivating Carrie, was malleable as putty in the hands of the potter. Fending off his clumsy advances, she explained wide-eyed that any kindness toward Roan was only for his having rescued her from possible danger on the runaway steed.

With effortless guile she bolstered Roan's resentment of Dunn, stoking the fires of jealousy, subtly revealing that the hapless Dunn whiled away countless hours at the gaming tables of the Saddle and Spur in Dodge City.

Provoked by Carrie's tearful lamentations, Roan would have challenged a stampeding buffalo herd to please her.

Roan was convinced that Dunn was the only obstacle between himself and the luscious Carrie. And so, blinded by raging passion that he didn't know would never be quenched, he headed for Dodge City and a showdown with Denver Dunn.

On his return to Buffalo Flats, Roan announced, "Well, we won't have to worry about him no more."

"Who?" Carrie said.

"That Dunn bastard. He's dead."

He watched her face turn from glowing pink to the color of ashes.

"That's what you wanted, ain't it?" he smirked.

Yes, she silently admitted, that was what she wanted. But she was not prepared for the stark reality of the deed. This man with his greedy leer had destroyed the father of her son.

Her knees went limp, and she was near to collapsing.

Roan reached out for her, but she pushed him away.

"Don't touch me!" she said.

Roan's crude advances had repulsed her from the beginning. She endured them only because she knew she could persuade him to free her from an unhappy marriage. Now she felt only revulsion, eager for him to be gone, suddenly conscience-stricken that she had allowed herself to become associated with such a ruthless monster.

"I want you to go, Aubrey."

"Go? Well, hell, Carrie—"

"Someone will be looking for you, and I don't want them to find you here."

"You mean the law?" he said with a cocky grin. "You got no reason to worry about the law. I got friends in high places."

"I'm sure you have, but I want you to go anyway."

"My brother is the law in Buffalo Flats."

"Your brother?"

"Castledine. Him and me had the same ma."

She could hardly breathe.

Roan was so busy waving his arms to convince her that Castledine was his brother that he missed the look of horror on her face.

Her body trembled as she marched to the door, threw it open, and told the seething Roan goodbye. He stormed out, having been rejected once again.

Carrie leaned heavily against the door, and covered her face with quivering hands.

She must give Roan no reason to suspect that it was because of his brother that she wanted Dunn out of the way. There was no way to predict what the hot-headed Aubrey might do if he learned about her and John.

She feared for her life, and Castledine's.

Her relationship with Castledine had begun only weeks before. Dunn's compulsion for gambling had driven her to take a job as a barmaid at the Dodge House in Dodge City. One Saturday night she served Castledine at suppertime, and was instantly attracted to the imposing figure and engaging manner of the handsome marshal from Buffalo Flats. For her, it was but a brief step from attending waitress to willing bed partner.

She soon left Dodge City for Buffalo Flats, taking with her what money she had been able to tuck away beyond the reach of the hapless Dunn.

Now, she feared her world was about to collapse. She slumped to the floor, buried her face in her hands, and wept.

Twenty-One

Savage watched the marshal's long strides carry him to where his black stallion was tethered in front of the Mercantile.

Castledine took a quick look around, then climbed into the saddle, and rode south.

At Savage's elbow, Cully said, "What's eatin' the marshal?"

"I don't know, but he was hell-bent to get some place." Savage kept an eye on the marshal until he disappeared at the end of the street. "He knows we're after Roan."

"Oh? Say, Will, I heard some feller mention Roan's name a while ago over at the boardin' house."

"How's that?"

"There was a couple of drummers shootin' the breeze, and one of 'em says a feller named Denver Dunn was killed in a poker game over at Dodge. Said some drifter name of Roan done it."

To Savage the news that Roan had killed again was not as great a shock as hearing the name of the man he killed. He'd had no idea that Dunn was in Dodge City, nor that he was even still alive.

"Are you certain of that, Amos?"

"I'm certain that's what the feller said."

Savage's mind was suddenly flooded with thoughts of Carrie. He could muster no sorrow for Denver Dunn, but, with

Dunn dead, maybe there was a some chance— No. Four years ago she had let him know that whatever she felt for him before was gone. He shoved the thought aside.

"Amos, it looks like Roan may have a time staying alive till we get to him."

He mulled that over while his eyes meandered down the street toward the stage office. They came to rest on a red-haired woman who some man was helping down from the coach. He was pretty sure he had seen her before.

He moved toward the stage office, and said to Amos, "I'll see you later."

By the time he got there, the woman was nowhere around.

To the brawny man unloading the luggage, he said, "Are you the stage driver?"

"Don't take no genius to figger that out," was the curt reply.

"That woman who just got off the stage—"

"Yeah? Nice looking lady."

"Do you know who she was?"

"She didn't say. I picked her up in Hays this morning. Long as she's got the fare, they don't pay me to be no damn detective. Anyways," he smirked, "them whores comes and goes. Here today and gone next week."

"What's your name, mister?"

"Orlie Potts. Twenty-two year I been—"

Savage cut him short with a blow to the mouth that sent the hulking Potts sprawling on his backside. Savage went after him with a headlong dive. Potts rolled away and scrambled to his feet. He kicked at Savage, and Savage grabbed his flying boot and twisted him to the ground. With a mad dog snarl, Potts lumbered to his feet and struck Savage a vicious right to the head that sent him reeling. Potts pummeled him with jabs to the midsection, and Savage sank to his knees. Potts knocked him over and pulled back a big fist to strike again, but Savage squirmed free. Potts stayed with him, winding up for a blow that would have put Savage away. But, Savage grabbed the fist with both hands and twisted the stage driver's arm until he fell back.

Savage bounced to his feet. Head-to-head they fought like angry bulls.

Potts flailed away with blows that didn't land. Savage worked his way inside the driver's long arms and jabbed a right to Orlie's head, a left to his flabby paunch, and a right fist to the mouth that put the burly Potts on the ground.

Savage rushed at him, but Potts waved a hand. He'd had enough.

"What's the trouble, Will?" It was Cully.

Savage kept a wary eye on Potts.

"He didn't have proper respect for women," he said.

Potts struggled to his feet, and grabbed his hat off the ground. He slapped it against his knee, creating a cloud of dust. With a vengeful glare at Savage, he plopped the hat on his head, and stumbled toward the stagecoach.

He climbed slack-jawed onto the driver's seat, took up the reins, and flicked the team into motion. The stage rumbled off down the street, and disappeared around the corner of the Mercantile.

"Uh-oh," Cully said. "Somethin's wrong with Henry."

The boy was dashing toward the two men, frantically waving his arms.

"Will!" he called. "Will Savage!"

"Hold on there, Henry," Savage said, grabbing his arm.

"It's Mama, Will. Can you come? She's bad sick."

Savage swung onto the mare tethered at the rail, and pulled Henry up behind him. He buried a spur in the horse's flank, and said to Amos, "Get hold of Doc Stark in Dodge and tell him to get out here as fast as he can."

Amos took off for the telegraph office.

Twenty-Two

What have you done, Aubrey?"

Castledine was trying not to explode in his brother's face.

"Nothin'," Aubrey whined. "I ain't done nothin'.

"A man rides all the way out here from Abilene looking for you, and you say you've done nothing?"

Being the older brother of Aubrey Roan had never been easy for John Castledine. Since Aubrey left school at fourteen he'd been nothing but trouble.

He had looked to John to rescue him from one scrape after another. When trouble found Roan, Roan found Castledine.

"I don't know no Will Savage," Aubrey said. "Heard of him. Some kind of gunslinger, what I hear."

Castledine paced the dirt floor of Aubrey's cluttered shack. There was no doubt in his mind that Aubrey had killed Joe Freeman. Castledine did question whether there was a reward for Freeman's killer. If there was a reward, he reasoned, it most likely would go to Savage for bringing in the killer. Somewhere between his lawman's badge and his family need to protect his outlaw brother lay a narrow line that, sooner or later, Castledine would have to cross.

Watching Roan nursing a half-empty whiskey bottle, Castledine searched for a reason why he wanted to protect him. There were limits to how far a man could go to shield even his brother from what was right. Why didn't he just tell Savage where Roan was and get it over with? It was only a matter of time before Savage would find him anyway. Upstanding, by-the-book lawman that he was, what kept Castledine from hauling Aubrey into town and turning him over to Savage?

Answers didn't come easy. Whatever else Roan had become, he was still his brother, and their dead mother would expect him to do whatever he could to save him.

"Did you kill Joe Freeman?"

"What?" Aubrey acted surprised.

"Joe Freeman, Aubrey. Did you kill him?"

Aubrey shrugged.

"I guess so," he said, like a child being scolded for spilling his milk.

"You guess so. Did you kill him or not?"

"I don't know, John. He come at me—"

"Don't lie to me, Aubrey!"

"Yeah!"

Roan threw up his hands. He knew there was no way to get around his brother's doggedness. He had never been a match for John, at any time at anything. John was always right.

Aubrey resented that. But he knew John wouldn't let up on him until he got the truth.

"I shot him!" It was hopeless to deny it.

"Did you kill him?"

"I lost my head."

The whining Aubrey collapsed against a pile of dingy quilts that he had rounded up for bed clothes.

"I didn't go to kill him," he said.

"You didn't go to kill him!" Castledine glared at him. "Why didn't you tell me this when you first showed up here? Why the hell did you show up here at all?"

"I didn't have no place else to go."

Castledine shoved a newspaper under his nose.

"What about this one, Aubrey?"

Aubrey glanced at the headline.

"Denver Dunn?" he said with child-like innocence. "Why, hell yes, I killed old Denver. He wasn't no good for nothin'. He was Carrie's husband, and she wanted to get rid of him."

"Carrie's husband?" How would Aubrey know that?

"Yeah. Carrie Dunn." He gave his brother an odd look. "You know Carrie?"

"I'm the town marshal. It's my job to know everybody."

Aubrey's reference to Carrie was quite casual. Castledine fought the notion that Aubrey and Carrie were spending time together. But then, Carrie had no money. How else could she have enticed Roan to kill for her?

"Let me tell you something, Aubrey," Castledine said. "You don't move out of this shack until I find out what's going on here. You just sit tight until I get back to you, or until hell freezes over, whichever comes first. Do you understand me, Aubrey?"

"Yeah, John, I hear you. Don't get all riled up."

"I don't want to see you in town again."

Since Aubrey was big enough to walk, he'd found ways to tie his older brother in knots. This time was no different.

The ride back to town gave Castledine time to unwind.

He hadn't told Aubrey about the reward because he was not convinced that there was one. What kind of judge would post a reward for killing a town marshal? Even if Savage's story made sense, Castledine wasn't sure he'd want Roan to know about it. He suspected that Savage spread word of the reward to lure Roan out of hiding.

He knew men like Savage. Savage would keep digging, kicking at stones, and poking his nose around until he got what he came for. If he found out he and Roan were born to the same mother, he would come at him like a bull at a red flag.

Castledine knew that one day he and Savage would have to settle things between them. It was not a time he looked forward to.

Twenty-Three

Sarah Wadsworth was crumpled on her front room floor.

"I tried to move her," Henry said with tearful eyes, "but I couldn't lift her."

Savage picked up Sarah's limp body and carried her to the bed.

"Sarah," he said. "Sarah?"

"So—hot," she said, feverishly moving her head from side to side. She yanked the pillow from under her head and flung it against the wall. "So—hot—so—dizzy."

Savage told Henry to bring a pan of cold water and some towels.

When Henry brought them, Savage began bathing Sarah's face, throat, and forehead. Her fever began to subside, and she lapsed into a troubled sleep. He could only watch and wait.

It was getting late, and Savage wondered what was keeping Doc Stark.

Would he get there in time to help Sarah?

"Will," Henry said, "is my mama gonna be all right?"

He told Henry that if his mother could sleep a while that was a good sign.

Henry knelt beside her bed, and kept a close watch on his mother's labored breathing.

"She don't look too good, does she, Will?"

Savage could think of nothing to say that would make the boy feel better.

By the time Doc Stark arrived shortly after sunset, Sarah had breathed her last. With a sorrowful look at Henry, he pulled the sheet up over her head.

Henry grabbed Savage around the waist, and buried his face in his chest.

Twenty-Four

John Castledine rolled his big body off Carrie Dunn.

"Do you want to tell me again, what Aubrey told you?" he said.

Carrie snuggled close to him, pressed her naked body against his. She caressed his cheek with her fingertips.

"It won't be any different than it was before," she said drowsily. "He bragged that his brother was the marshal in Buffalo Flats."

Castledine studied the rough-hewn logs of the ceiling, as though looking for answers. He didn't find them.

"Were you surprised?" he said.

"It scared the hell out of me."

"Why?"

"Because, if Aubrey knew you and I were—"

"Yes? You and I were what?"

"I was afraid of what he might do. You know what a hothead he is. I was afraid he'd kill us both."

"Were you sleeping with him?"

"Aubrey?" She was startled by the question. "No, I never slept with Aubrey."

"Tell me the truth."

"That is the truth, John. He pushed me to all the time, but I never did."

"Then what was your interest in him?"

Castledine knew the answer, but he was curious whether she would admit it.

"I told you. He rescued me from a runaway horse."

"That's all?"

"Hell, John, if I wanted to sleep with him I could have."

She was beginning to whine like Aubrey.

"Did you set it up for Aubrey to kill Denver Dunn in that poker game?"

"What poker game?"

"Don't play games with me, Carrie. I know Aubrey killed Dunn in a poker game at the Saddle and Spur in Dodge City. Now, did you set it up or not?"

She broke down.

"I did it for you, John," she sobbed. "For you and me. I thought you'd be glad he was gone."

"You didn't have to kill him."

"Denver was no good. I never loved him. He tricked me into marrying him."

Castledine rolled out of bed and reached for his clothes.

"That was no reason to kill him."

"He wouldn't let me go. He threatened to kill me if I ever left him."

Castledine buckled his gun belt, pressed his hat on, and stepped to the door.

Carrie bolted from the bed, pleading, "John, please! I love you!"

He pushed her aside.

"You were wrong, Carrie. This time it was different."

The door closed, and he was gone.

Alone and heartbroken, never had she felt such sorrow. She'd lost Savage four years ago, and now Castledine cast her aside. She was good enough only for Aubrey, and she detested him.

In her wretchedness she longed to be again at Blanchard's General Store back in Abilene where she and Will first met.

"Why would he want to have anything to do with a heifer like me now," she moaned, "after the wreck I've made of my life?"

She would not have believed that for four years Savage had lived with the hope of being with her again.

Twenty-Five

Doc Stark was a wiry little old man with gray eyebrows as bushy as the mustache that sagged at the ends. In his black suit, white broadcloth shirt, and black string tie, his wrinkled countenance reflected the pain of a lifetime of watching people die.

He placed a stubby-fingered hand under the elbow of the tall cowboy beside him, and guided him to a corner of Sarah Wadsworth's front room.

"Are you the boy's daddy?" Doc said.

"No. Just a friend. Will Savage."

"Do you know who is his daddy?"

"He was killed in a stage holdup years ago."

"Were you keeping company with his mama?"

"What are you getting at, Doc?"

"Well, I'm more than a little concerned about what's going to happen to that boy now that his mama's gone."

Friends and neighbors had come to see what they could do to comfort Henry in his time of sorrow. Across the room, Savage saw Henry being comforted by the Reverend and Mrs. Wesley Hale of the white-steepled church in Buffalo Flats.

"So am I, Doc." Savage nodded toward Henry. "It looks to me like he's in pretty good hands."

"Those people have got more than they can take care of already," Doc said. "They don't need another mouth to feed."

With a solemn look, he said, "Why don't you take him on, Savage?"

Savage squirmed. "Now, wait a minute, Doc. I think a heap of that boy, but I'm not cut out to be a daddy to him."

"Now, you just hold on, Savage. You're shakier than a nervous rattler. I don't think you understand what's at stake here. With some schooling and proper upbringing that boy could amount to something."

"You just tipped your hand, Doc, when you said proper upbringing. That's something I can't give him. I've never been a daddy, and I don't figure to start in now."

"Well, for some reason he puts a good deal of stock in whatever it is he sees in you. If you gave it a chance—"

"I can't do it, Doc. It's not fair to Henry to even talk about it. He's just lost his mama, and he hasn't had a daddy since he was little. He deserves better than being toted around all over creation by a man who's no kin." Savage gave his head a dogged shake. "No, sir, it wouldn't work, and I'm not giving it a chance to fail."

Doc raked his fuzzy chin with a fist, and pinned Savage with a steady gaze.

"You're a stubborn man, Will Savage," he said. "A mighty stubborn man."

Savage responded with a broad grin. He watched Doc move across the room and place a comforting arm across the shoulders of Henry Wadsworth.

Savage felt sorry for the boy, and shared Doc's concern for him, but he was sure Henry would be better off living with some family.

Before he left the next morning, Doc Stark sent wires to friends in Dodge City, and arranged for a childless couple to give Henry a home.

"They'll take good care of you, Henry," he said. "I know these people. They'll see that you get some schooling, and make a good home for you."

"Yes, sir," said the tearful Henry.

He didn't want to go. He wanted to stay with Will Savage, but he figured the doctor knew what was best for him.

Twenty-Six

Savage helped Henry collect his few belongings, packed them in a small valise, and tied it with a cotton cord around the middle.

"I talked to Mr. Stone at the bank about your mother's place, Henry," Savage said. "He'll be getting in touch with you about that."

"Why do I have to go to Dodge, Will?"

"Because I can't do for you what these folks can. You need a home, and they need a boy."

At the stage office, Orlie Potts was groaning under the weight of a trunk he was loading on the stagecoach.

Henry climbed aboard and sat next to the window. His damp eyes were focused on Savage.

"Are you gonna come see me in Dodge?" Henry said.

"You bet, Henry. You get settled in, and study hard, and I'll be seeing you almost before you know it."

Henry sniffled and wiped his eyes.

Savage tossed Henry's bag to the sweating Potts.

"You take good care of this boy, Orlie," he said.

"I don't have to be told that," Potts shot back. He climbed onto the driver's seat, grabbed a handful of reins, and threw off the brake. "For twenty-two year I been—" His voice trailed off as he flicked the lines, and the stagecoach lunged forward.

Henry stuck his head out the window and waved to Savage until he could no longer see him. Neither of them could have known that Henry would never make it to Dodge City.

Savage turned away and saw Castledine riding south again. He was curious to find out why.

Twenty-Seven

For the first mile or so, Castledine let the black pick his way south across the dry prairie, then spurred him into an easy canter. Mounting a knoll overlooking a swale, he paused for a look around. He knew where he was. He had been there before, but instinct prompted him to check to see whether he had been followed.

A quarter mile beyond the swale stood an old shack half hidden by a stand of sycamores. Beside the shack a huge roan stallion was tethered to a limb, pawing at the parched earth. Castledine knew who was in that shack, and didn't look forward to another round with his errant brother.

Even so, he kept coming back, hoping to find something about Aubrey that was worth salvaging. Castledine pulled up beside the shack, dropped a rein over a limb, and strode toward the door without a backward glance.

From behind a clump of evergreens, Savage watched the marshal go inside, then wheeled his mare toward town.

Twenty-Eight

Orlie Potts lumbered around the way station, herding his charges toward the stagecoach.

"Hurry it up!" he yelled. "We gotta be cloppin' dirt in three minutes!"

Counting heads, Orlie came up one short.

"Where's that boy?" he growled at no one in particular.

"What boy?" said the moon-faced drummer in the black derby.

"The one that got on at Buffalo Flats. Skinny kid with sandy hair."

"Oh, you mean he's gone?" said the fat lady in the green gingham dress.

"He was here when we stopped."

"I know, lady," Orlie grumbled. "That's why I'm lookin' for him now."

He muttered his way back into the station, and yelled at Jess Wall, the station master.

"Did you see that skinny kid that got off the stage a few minutes ago?"

"No skinny kid came in here, Orlie. Did you lose one?"

Potts ignored him and turned away. He stomped out behind the log building and threw open the door to the privy. Finding no boy, he banged the door shut.

"Hey, boy!" he called at the top of his voice. He cast a few anxious glances left and right, then called again. "Hey you, boy! Where the hell are you? Come on, the stage is pullin' out!"

Henry was crouched behind a small rise fifty yards beyond the station. He flattened out on his belly, and kept a sharp eye on the frustrated stagecoach driver. He hoped Orlie wouldn't venture that far.

"Hey you, boy!" Orlie shouted one last time. "You out there? We're leavin'!"

Orlie waited for a moment, looking, listening. Seeing nothing, hearing nothing, he turned back, worried.

"Go on ahead," Henry was thinking real hard. "Get on outa here. I ain't goin' with you. I ain't goin' to no Dodge with you or anybody else. Ain't nothin' in Dodge for me."

"Jess," Orlie said in a sweat, one foot out the door. "I want you to make a full report of this. If that boy don't show up, my ass is in a sling. You know I tried to find him, and I want you to be damn sure to make a note of that in your report."

"Oh I will, Orlie, yes, sir," Jess said. "Don't you worry about a thing. I'll take care of it for you, yes, sir."

Orlie took off and climbed aboard the coach. He was hot under the collar, but half scared too. All passengers were his responsibility, and in twenty- two years he had never lost one.

Henry scrunched down behind the hill until he heard Orlie yell, "Big'un! Blue!"

The lines whacked, the team lunged forward, and the stagecoach careened off out of sight, bound for Dodge City.

When he thought it was safe, Henry stood up and took a look around. Satisfied that the stage was really gone, and that nobody was looking for him, he checked his bearings, and started walking with his face to the sun.

How far the stage had brought him, Henry had no idea, but he struck out at a brisk pace, determined to make it back to Buffalo Flats. He told himself that all he had to do was follow the stage road, and it would lead him right back to where he wanted to be. With Will Savage.

Sweat from the scorching sun soon soaked his thin cotton shirt and pants. His mouth was dry as a burnt oak leaf. In his haste to escape the searching eyes of Orlie Potts, Henry had thought of neither food nor water. All he had were the clothes on his back.

He began to think that leaving the stage was not such a good idea after all. But, living with some strange family in Dodge City wasn't what he wanted either. He was sure that if he could make it back to Buffalo Flats, Will would take care of him.

His empty stomach growled, and the stifling mid-day heat was sapping the strength from his young body. With wobbly steps and bleary eyes, he began to waver from the stage road, and soon could no longer follow its tracks.

He dragged a sleeve across his sweaty face. How much longer could he stay on his feet? Maybe he should have gone on to Dodge with Orlie. Maybe living with that family wouldn't be so bad as he'd thought. If he could just rest for a little while he'd feel better. But there was no place to rest, not even a tree for shade. Anyway, if he should stop, wolves and coyotes and rattlers, and all kinds of evil things might attack him, ripping his flesh, eating him alive! Oh, he began to sniffle, why had he left that stagecoach? Why did his mama have to die and leave him to face the world all alone? Why couldn't he just— He collapsed face down on the dry earth.

Twenty-Nine

Savage elbowed his way around punchers at the Last Dog
Saloon, and spotted Amos at a poker table in the corner. Amos
was trying to decipher the blank expressions on the faces of the
four other players shielding their cards behind cupped hands.
Savage was headed for a visit with Amos when he heard
somebody call his name.

"Hey, Will Savage!"

Savage spun around and saw Charlie Crum with his hand
stuck out across the bar. Savage grasped it in a hardy
handshake.

"I wondered where you were, Charlie," he said.

"I laid out a while. I've got me some help now." The
bushy white mane and deep ridges in his leathery face marked
Crum's seventy-odd years. He nodded at the chunky, balding
man at the end of the bar. "Jimmy here spells me from time to
time." Charlie paused, then said,. "Somebody said you cleared
a batch of garbage out of my place while I was gone."

"The Barefoots?"

Crum nodded. "They've been needing that for a while."
His face crinkled into a smile. "You gonna be around, Will?"

"I'll be around."

"Too bad about the Wadsworth woman. Is that boy doing
all right?"

"Henry's on his way to Dodge. Doc Stark found a place for him with a family there."

"Leave it to old Doc to put him in good hands."

Savage looked away.

He saw a woman chatting with some men at a table across the room. She was wearing a bright green dress and high-heeled red slippers. A mass of gleaming red hair was piled on top of her head.

A slow remembering smile sneaked across his thin lips. In all his born days, he'd never seen a more perfect sitter than the one upon which his eyes now rested.

Meg McGraff had come to town.

Savage glanced back at the grinning Charlie Crum. He knew what Charlie was thinking.

"That's Meg all right, Will. She just got in."

Savage eased over and tapped that lady on the shoulder. She whirled around and shrieked, "Will Savage, you old sidewinder!"

"Howdy, Meg."

She threw her arms around his neck and planted a kiss squarely on his mouth.

Envious cowboys hooted. Savage turned red.

"How'd you know I was here?" Meg said.

"I saw you get off the stage," Savage said. "Run you out of Hays, did they?"

"Oh, no, Charlie sent for me. He said he needed help keeping you big ol' dry-tongued cowpokes in line."

"I'm glad to see you, Meg."

Her sidelong look from the tops of her green eyes told him she too remembered.

"Old times and good friends are not forgotten," she said, cocking her head to one side. "Any time, Savage. Any time."

Savage moved away to the poker table, and caught Amos's eye. He motioned with his head toward the door, then moved that way.

Amos checked his poker hand, then tossed it onto the pot in the middle of the table.

"Deal me out," he said, and followed Savage outside.

Savage waited for him at the hitch rail.

Cully said, "I wondered what happened to you."

"I found out where that marshal's been riding to."

"Yeah?"

"About six miles south of town there's a knob-headed rise that looks down into a little valley. There's an old line shack back among some sycamores, and that's where I followed the marshal to."

"You follered him?"

Savage nodded.

"He strolled right into that shack and never looked back. Another thing, Amos. There was a big old roan stallion tied beside that shack. Like the one you and Cap'n Billy told me about."

"Be damned, Will! Reckon the marshal knowed who was in there?"

"He had to know. Why else would he be riding out there?"

"Looks like there's a skunk in the woodpile somewheres, don't it?"

"I figured there must be some connection between Castledine and Roan, and it wouldn't be smart to bust in on the two of them."

"You coulda woke up dead."

"Castledine let on to me like he never heard of Roan, and now he's riding out to that shack where Roan is holed up."

"If he's in cahoots with the marshal, why'd Roan be hidin' out, Will?"

"Roan knows he killed Joe Freeman. And there's that Dunn killing too. He's got a reason to hide out. The strange thing is, Castledine knows Roan killed Freeman. Yet he claims he knows nothing about him."

"It don't make no sense—the marshal ridin' out there to that shack, unless he knew Roan was in it. And if he knew, why wouldn't he be tellin' you?"

Savage searched for an answer that made sense. He couldn't come up with one.

"Back in Junction City," he said, changing the subject, "there's a banker hell-bent to get his hands on my ranch. I owe him money, and unless I can come up with a thousand dollars by the first of the month, he's threatening to foreclose on me. I could lose it all if I don't get to Roan"

He looked off toward the marshal's office, trying to fit the pieces of the puzzle together.

He had scraped and borrowed to get his ranch to where it was beginning to pay off, and he wasn't going to lose it because of some shenanigans between the law and an outlaw. Still, if Castledine was half the lawman Savage believed him to be, why would he be hob-nobbing with the man he had come to find?

To Amos, he said, "I'd hate to have to go through Castledine to get to Roan."

"You mean to deliver the reward?"

"Half of it's mine. The thousand dollars I need to get Hogan off my back."

"Does Castledine know about the reward?"

"He knows, but he says nobody deserves a reward for killing a lawman."

"It still don't make no sense he'd be ridin' out there to pay Roan a visit."

"There's your skunk in the woodpile, Amos."

"Maybe the best way to handle this is to ride out there, give Roan the money, and see where the chips fall."

"That's a fine notion, except that Roan doesn't know he's got the money coming."

"Well, that's right. And if you started talkin' to him about killin' Freeman, he's likely to exercise his right as a red-blooded American asshole and blow your head off."

Savage nodded.

"Be damned if I wouldn't in his place!" Amos said.

Savage let that soak in.

"I think it's time for another visit with the marshal," he said, moving away. Then, he stopped, and said, "When this is over, do you want to come back with me?"

"To Junction City?" Savage nodded, and Amos grinned. "Be damned, Savage!"

Thirty

Henry knew he had lost his hat because it wasn't blocking his view of the chunky old man kneeling on the ground beside him. He had no idea how long he had lain in the sun. He remembered being hungry and thirsty. His knees felt like they were made of rubber.

But his mind was clear enough now as he gulped the cool water from the canteen he was clutching with both hands.

The man looked old enough to be his grandfather if he'd had one. He had white lamb chop whiskers and a drooping white mustache. Wiry yellow hairs stuck out from his nostrils, and on his pitted nose rested a pair of wire-rimmed spectacles. His denim pant legs were stuffed into the tops of black boots, and around his left wrist hung a leather riding crop.

With his right hand, the old man was holding Henry's head off the ground.

"Not too much just now, boy," the man said, taking the canteen away.

"Can you ride?"

"I—I—don't know," Henry stammered. "I—why—I—"

"Easy, son, easy." To someone Henry couldn't see, the man called, "Jubal."

A boy about Henry's age stepped forward and placed Henry's hat on his head.

"We found it back a ways," the old man said.

He helped Henry to a sitting position. Henry noticed there were others in the group, some as old as the man kneeling beside him, and some younger. They all wore stern expressions on their sunburned faces. Ten or twelve of them, Henry guessed, sitting their mounts, solemnly watching the old man. Like they didn't know what to do until he told them to do it. Dusty, trail weary men and boys, saddle scabbards strapped to sweaty, heavy breathing mounts that had been ridden many miles. Revolvers were laced to faded Levi's. Even the younger ones, some as young as Henry, carried guns or rifles, and all eyes focused on him.

"Get some grub for the boy," the old man said.

The boy Jubal who had brought his hat fetched a can of beans and some hardtack.

Henry wolfed down the food, and gulped more water from the canteen.

"What's your name, son?" the old man said.

"Henry," he said around a mouthful of beans. "Henry Wadsworth."

"Where are you going, Henry?"

"Buffalo Flats."

Henry was too busy eating to note the sudden movement among the riders.

"That's where we're going too," said the old man. "Maybe, Henry Wadsworth, you'd like to ride along with us."

"Yes, sir, I would," Henry said.. "I truly would."

"Do your mama and daddy live in Buffalo Flats?"

"No, sir, they're dead."

"You got kin there, Henry?"

"No, sir, no kin. Just Will."

"Will?"

"Will Savage."

The old man stared with a peculiar smile at those who watched and listened.

Henry wondered why they stirred in their saddles.

Thirty-One

Jim Whitley never wanted to take that long hot ride to Buffalo Flats. He was getting too old to go chasing off to hell and gone after some hotheaded renegade. Even if he brought Roan back to stand trial, that wouldn't add one minute to the life of an old war horse who would rather be back in Abilene stuffing himself with his daughter's cooking, beating his son-in-law at checkers, and tossing his grandkids in the air to make them laugh. But, unable to make a deal with Savage, he'd had no choice, except to sweat out that ride in search of Aubrey Roan.

Whitley's first stop in his search for Roan had been a visit with the sheriff at Colby. The sheriff told him about Roan's pistol-whipping a man in a poker game.

"He knows he's not welcome back here," the sheriff said. "The last I knew, he was headed toward Buffalo Flats."

Whitley had nosed around Buffalo Flats, studying faces, listening to voices, observing the actions of people he saw coming and going. Hoping for some sign that would help him sniff out Roan's trail. He spotted Savage time or two, but decided to steer clear of him for the time being.

He knew who Castledine was, but avoided him until he had some notion where his nose would lead him.

Oddly, it was Castledine who pointed Whitley to the end of his search.

Whitley had uncovered nothing of value until one day, on his way out the back door of the Last Dog Saloon, he heard angry voices off to his right.

Such talk was common among raw-hiding punchers, and he thought little of what he heard. He was about to move on when he recognized one of the two men as Marshal John Castledine. The marshal was standing at the bottom of the stairway leading up to the rooms above the saloon. A younger man was facing him from half way up the stairs.

"Aubrey," Whitley heard the marshal say, with little success to control the level of his voice. "What the hell are you doing here?"

Whitley eased back into the shadows, ground out his cigarette with the toe of his boot, and listened.

Slowly the younger man slouched back down the stairs, and stopped a few feet in front of the marshal.

"I was just coming to see Carrie, John," he said,

"Coming to see Carrie," Castledine seethed. "Didn't I tell you to stay put till I got back to you?"

"Yeah, John," Aubrey whined. "But, I been holed up out there so long— I need to talk to somebody."

Castledine's patience was fading fast. He took a deep breath to calm his anger.

"All right," Castledine said. "Go on back out there, and I'll see you tonight.And, Aubrey."

"Yeah, John?"

"Stay away from Carrie." His eyes bore into the face of his whimpering brother. "Did Carrie pay you to kill Denver Dunn?"

"Naw, he wasn't no good for nothin'. It was just another killin', John."

"Is that all it was to you—just another killing? Let me tell you something, Aubrey. You better be damn careful what you do around here, or I'll come after you myself, brother or no brother. Do you understand me, Aubrey?"

"Yeah, John, I hear you."

"Now, get on back out there. And don't make a move till you see me coming."

On his way into the back door of the Last Dog, Castledine nodded to an old puncher whose face was covered with his hands, lighting a cigarette.

Jim Whitley stepped aside to let him pass.

Aubrey waited until his brother disappeared into the Last Dog, then bounded up the back stairs in a blind rage.

"Big tough marshal!" he muttered. "Who the hell does he think he's messin' with?"

Thirty- Two

Henry was riding up behind a young man he heard someone call Bradley. Bradley wore his six-shooter slung low on his right thigh, tied with a leather thong like a gunslinger's. Henry noticed that Bradley grinned a lot, even when there was nothing to grin about.

He heard Bradley call the old man Daddy. Bradley was riding on Daddy's left. To his right rode another old man Bradley called Uncle Silas. The ancient weapon Uncle Silas carried looked to Henry like a squirrel gun.

All the men wore pleasant expressions, except for Daddy. Daddy was stern faced and serious. He looked neither right nor left, like he had something pushing to do and couldn't wait to get it done. Daddy set the pace with a steady gait. Henry wondered what was so urgent.

Uncle Silas was skinny and wrinkle-faced. Henry thought he looked like he would rather be home digging turnips. Uncle Silas leaned forward and looked past Henry and Bradley to Daddy.

"Angus," Uncle Silas said, "what we doing this for?"

"Because," Daddy said, "he killed our kin."

"We don't know what the partic'lars was," Uncle Silas said. "For all we know, it coulda been a fair fight."

"Coulda been," Angus said, but he didn't care.

"Well, then what we doing this for?"

"How long you know me, Silas?"

"Thirty-eight year."

"Ever since you took my sister Ellie for a wife. I didn't like you then, and I don't like you now."

"Now, you just hold on there, Angus Barefoot!"

Barefoot. Barefoot? Barefoot!

A lightning streak of fear ripped Henry's young body.

"When a man kills my boys," Angus said, looking straight ahead, "I don't wait to find out the fair of it. He killed them. That's all I need to know."

"We ain't gunfighters," Silas complained. "We be farmers. What do we know about shooting and killing?"

Angus swiveled his head for a look at Bradley.

"Bradley here," he said with a half smile."He'll do our killing. Ain't that right, son?"

Bradley flashed a simple grin, but didn't answer.

Henry took his arms from around Bradley's waist. He was scared for Savage.

Thirty-Three

Savage was in a hurry. He knew where to find Roan. It was time to settle with him, and get back to Junction City before Hogan decided he wasn't coming. Cinching his saddle, something kept gnawing at him about Castledine. Why had the marshal ridden out to that shack where Roan was hiding? What was the connection between Castledine and Roan?

Castledine had known from the beginning where Roan was, so why had he let on like he didn't know?

Leading the mare out of the livery, Savage was surprised to see Jim Whitley riding his way.

"I bet you thought you'd seen the last of me," Whitley said with a secret smile, like he knew something nobody else knew. And he did. He was eager to share the news with Will Savage.

"You're right, I did," Savage said.

"I know you're a man born to the saddle, bred to life in the wide open spaces, but I wouldn't take this ride again for my own burying."

Whitley let his glance slide over the area to make sure no one else was within earshot.

"The fact is," he said, "I stumbled onto something I knew you'd want to know." He took a step closer, and said in a low voice, "Savage, did you know Aubrey Roan is a brother to John Castledine?"

"His brother?" Savage swallowed hard. "Are you certain of that?"

"My guess is they're half brothers, with the same mother."

"How did you learn that?"

"I heard these two fellows talking behind the saloon. One of them was Castledine, and he called the other one Aubrey. Castledine said, you better be damn careful, Aubrey, or I'll come after you myself—brother or no brother."

"You're sure it was Roan he was talking to?"

"It was Roan all right. I've seen him around Abilene enough to know what he looks like."

Answers were coming in bunches. Savage knew now why Castledine had been so interested in who was in that shack, and why the marshal had balked at helping him locate Roan. Castledine hadn't come close to pointing him toward his errant brother.

"It looks like we've got ourselves a little thicker pot of stew," Savage said.

He chewed on that for a minute.

"Why are you telling me about this, Mr. Whitley, instead of making your own move?"

"Well, you know, Savage, when a man gets a little age on him," Whitley said with a sheepish grin, "he starts getting a little cautious. He'd like to be around for his sixtieth birthday, maybe spend more time with his kids and grand kids."

"Yeah."

"I'm pushing sixty, and the fire in my belly is not as hot as it once was. When a man gets too cautious he'd better hang 'em up, or he could wind up dead."

Savage studied the creases in the old puncher's leathery face.

"Castledine?" he said.

"There was a time," Whitley said with that little grin sneaking across his face, "when I'd have challenged either of those two, or both of them at once if need be, but not today. My time has passed."

Savage had thought of the same thing. He wasn't as old as Whitley, but he didn't plan on waiting until he was before he put his guns away. This Roan caper would be his last. Once he got back to Junction City, he meant to spend the rest of his life poking cattle on that ranch of his.

"I don't blame an old war horse like you for cashing in his chips," he said. "Most of us don't know when it's time to quit until it's too late."

"To tell the truth, with you on his trail, I know Roan won't get away with anything. Otherwise, I'd have to take that other fork in the road."

Savage grasped Whitley's hand, then watched him ride east.

Savage turned away and caught sight of the building with the sign on the front that said, "Marshal's Office."

"Damn you, Castledine!"

Thirty-Four

A scruffy buckskin mare ambled down the middle of the dusty street. Atop the mare was perched a lanky, unshaven man in a ragged cotton coat and a crow-picked black hat. In a toneless, high-pitched voice, he was singing:

"I eat when I'm hungry, I drink when I'm dry

"If a tree don't fall on me I'll live till I die

"If buzzards could teach me I'd know how to fly

"If hades was heaven I'd live in the sky."

Amos was climbing the steps to the Last Dog Saloon, itching to get inside and ante up. He was on a winning streak and didn't want to break it.

But his eyes were drawn to the buckskin, and the skinny rider with no chin.

Amos watched him shoot a stream of tobacco juice at an ant crawling up the hitching post in front of the Mercantile. The ant curled into a ball and dropped off the post, fell to the ground, and moved no more.

"Hey there, mister!" the skinny one said, pulling up in front of Amos. "You know a man name of Savage?"

Amos squinted for a better look at the scroungy stranger grinning at him with a simple look on his face.

"Mebbe," Amos said. He looked past the stranger to where Savage was mounting up near the livery stable and had just watched Jim Whitley ride away.

"Got a message for him," the skinny one said to Amos. He held up a scrap of brown paper. "It says Mr. Will Savage, Buffalo Flats. Can you tell me where to start lookin' for him?"

Amos was puzzled as to what kind of message this scraggly-assed looney could have for Will Savage.

"Are you pressed for time?" Amos said.

"No, sir. I got nothin' to do till I get shut of this piece of paper, then I'll be headin' back."

"Back where?"

"Out yonder," the man said with a jerk of his head.

Amos got a queasy feeling that what the message said Savage would not want to hear.

"Why are you goin' back out yonder?" he said.

"'Cause that's where we've got him."

"Where you got who?"

"Henry Wadsworth." He was losing patience.

For an uneasy moment Amos studied the face of the gawky rider, trying to read the meaning of what he said.

"You got Henry?"

"Yeah, I told you once."

"You wait right there," Amos said. He took off after Savage on the run.

Savage drew rein when he heard Amos call to him.

"Some feller ridin' in," Amos said. With his eyes he indicated the skinny man on the buckskin.

"I see him."

"He sys he's got a message for you." Amos took a deep breath. "They got Henry, Will."

"Henry? Henry's on his way to Dodge."

"That feller says they got him."

Savage wheeled the mare toward the waiting stranger. He leaped out of the saddle and said, "I'm Savage. What's this about a message?"

"Pleased to meet you," the man said with a grin, holding out the paper.

Savage grabbed it and read the scrawled first line: "We got Henry."

He glared at the scrawny messenger, and demanded, "What the hell does this mean?"

"Did you see the part down at the bottom where it says 'spectfully signed by Angus Barefoot?'"

Savage's eyes went back to the note. Incensed by what it said, he hauled the grinning scarecrow off the buckskin and flung him to the ground. He grabbed him by the coat collar and pulled him to his feet, then backhanded him across the mouth.

"You slimy bastard!" Savage seethed. "Where have you got Henry?"

"I can't tell you," the man wailed. He threw up his arms to ward off more blows.

Savage tightened his grip on the shabby coat collar, and the man's green eyes started bugging out. Savage drew back a fist to strike him again.

He felt a heavy hand on his shoulder, and heard an authoritative voice behind him.

"Let him go."

It was John Castledine.

Savage wasn't ready to let up on the rattle-boned stranger.

"Let him go, Savage," Castledine said.

Savage eased his grip and shoved the man to the ground.

"They've got Henry," he said to Castledine.

"I know." The marshal held up the crumpled note he retrieved from where it fell on the ground. "You won't learn anything this way."

Castledine's dark eyes scanned the area for anyone who might have come with the skinny rider. Satisfied that he was alone, he said to Savage, "If this man doesn't return by a certain time, you may never see Henry again."

Slowly the stranger lifted himself off the ground. He grabbed up his hat and plopped it on his head, warily eying Savage.

"What's your name?" Castledine said.

"Harley Barefoot."

Savage caught Castledine's eye. He knew what the marshal was thinking: "You could start a young war," he had warned.

To Harley Barefoot, Castledine said, "When are you supposed to be back?"

"Sundown." He wiped his face with a fistful of polkadot bandanna, and nodded at Savage. "I'm s'posed to braing him with me."

Castledine checked the sun. To Barefoot, he said, "What would they say to trading you for the boy?"

"Naw, that wouldn't do no good." His simple grin returned. "They don't care nothin' 'bout me. I'm just 'dopted. That's why they sent me. I ain't blood Barefoot."

Savage said, "Castledine."

The marshal took three steps and fell in beside Savage. Together they walked beyond the hearing of the curiosity seekers. Among them were the mayor and his cronies. As the two walked away they heard Castledine say, "I told you I'd throw you in jail if it came to this."

"Well, I didn't start this fight," Savage said, "and throwing me in jail won't end it."

The onlookers waited while the two talked. They saw them scan the open prairie to the east, gesturing, and nodding their heads.

Huddling with the marshal, Savage said, "There's only one way to handle this."

"How's that?"

"I've got to go out there and face them."

"There's no telling how many there are."

"No matter. They won't be satisfied until they get me for Henry. I can't let them hurt that boy."

Castledine checked the lowering sun again. "Not much time."

Savage had a time taking his eyes off the marshal's face. He fought the urge to have it out with him there and then. "Why the hell didn't you tell me Aubrey Roan was your brother?"

That's what he wanted to hit him with. Get down to it, and get it done.

But, there were more pressing matters to settle first. Henry's safety had to be taken care of. There would be time later for challenging the marshal.

"You may be right, Savage?" Castledine said. "But, it would be one man against who knows how many."

"They want my hide, so I'll take it to them."

Savage turned on a heel, and led the marshal back to the covey of curious surrounding the stringy Barefoot.

Savage swung into the saddle.

"Come on, Barefoot," he said. "Let's go get it done."

He nodded to Amos and traded looks with Castledine as he fell in beside Harley Barefoot and rode away without a backward glance.

Amos fidgeted and made a move as if to follow.

Castledine said, "I don't think he'd want you to do that, Mr. Cully."

Amos glared at the marshal, and drew an uneasy hand across his face.

They watched the two riders disappear beyond the horizon.

Thirty-Five

Aubrey Roan had scrambled up the back stairway and burst through the door on his way to room 203.

"Just because he's the oldest don't mean he's big enough to push me around," he muttered. "Tell me what to do, will he? Hah! I'll show him. Big brother! Big tough marshal!"

At the door of room 203 he tried the knob. The door was locked. He pounded on it until his bare knuckles hurt.

"Let me in, Carrie!"

The door opened a crack. Carrie showed him half her face.

"Oh, it's you," she said.

"Yeah, it's me." He pushed past her into the room.

"What do you want?" she spat, letting him know he wasn't welcome.

"Don't hassle me, Carrie. I've been pushed around enough for one day."

"Oh? Has little Aubrey been a bad boy again?"

"Shut up, Carrie!"

"Don't you tell me to shut up, you whimpering pup!"

"John knows about Denver."

Roan paced across the room and back, waving his arms in a wild motion.

That Castledine knew about Dunn's killing came as no surprise to Carrie, since John had dragged it out of her. Even so, she couldn't be too careful.

David Estes

Her relationship with Castledine was over, but there was no telling what the hotheaded Aubrey might do if he knew she and John had been lovers.

To throw him off guard, she showed him a shocked expression.

"John ain't no dummy," Roan said. "And he's always right." He turned on her, eyes flashing. "I don't like him knowin' what we done to Denver."

Carrie knew that the best way to deal with Aubrey was with brass. Boldness also bolstered her courage.

"We didn't do anything to Denver, Aubrey. You did. You're a big boy now. It's time you started acting like one."

"If John knows it was a set up—"

"You should have thought of that before," she said spitefully. "Denver's dead. It's too late to worry about it now."

"Yeah," Roan said, leering. "You got what you wanted, now how about what I want?"

He grabbed at the thin white coverlet that hid none of the tantalizing curves whose pleasures she had denied him.

She slipped away beyond his reach, and paused by the window overlooking the street. She peered out the window, and said, "Don't be such a little boy, Aubrey."

"Boy, hell!" He made a threatening move toward her. "I got Denver, now I get you!"

She put her hand out. "Wait!" she said.

On the street below she saw people scurrying about, forming a circle around some commotion in front of the Last Dog Saloon. Two men, one gawky and ill kempt in tattered clothing. The other man, taller, appeared to be angry. He jerked the smaller man off his horse and flung him to the ground.

"Who is that?" she said to Aubrey.

Aubrey didn't care what was taking place beyond the walls of Carrie's boudoir, but to appease her he slouched to the window and took a quick look. He saw the bigger man backhand the other across the mouth, then turned away without interest.

"Just a coupla likkered up punchers goin' at it," he said.

111

"No," Carrie said, catching her breath. "The tall one. He looks like—"

With a hand to her mouth, her lips silently formed the words, "Will Savage!"

"Come on, Carrie," Roan said. "I ain't got all day."

"No! Stay away from me!"

"Stay away from you?" His eyes narrowed, his lips curled in anger. "That's what John said. Why would my brother tell me to stay away from you?"

"I don' t know, Aubrey. How would I know why your big brother does anything?"

"Has John been comin' here?"

He grabbed at her, but she stepped away.

"He has, hasn't he?" Aubrey said.

"Get out of here, Aubrey!"

He grabbed her by an arm and shoved her across the room. She fell against the bedpost and crumpled to the floor.

"You whoring little bitch!" Roan roared.

He stormed out of the room and banged the door behind him.

Carrie lay where he left her, sobbing into her folded arms.

"Will Savage," she breathed, wishing he could hear her.

But even if he had heard her, why would he care about her now?

That time four years ago when he came looking for her— Why hadn't he swept her into his arms and carried her away? Oh, she would have fought like a cornered wildcat, of course. She wouldn't have wanted him to know how happy she was to see him, nor how she had longed to be free of Denver Dunn. But she had bared her teeth and sent him away.

Her heart had ached for Will after he rode away that day. How she had wished he had settled the score with Dunn and taken her with him. In her private moments she had viewed herself in the mirror, turning this way and that, caressing her hair with a soft palm, wanting to look her best when Will came back for her, though fearful that he never would.

Oh, why had she been such a fool as to let him go, instead of letting him know how miserable her life was without him?

Now, suddenly there he was. On the street in Buffalo Flats. She wanted to run to him and throw herself at his feet with half the town watching. Her heart cried out for her to beg him to take her back. But then, she told herself that Will could never love the shambles that she had made of her life.

"Oh, Will," she moaned. "Will, Will, Will!"

Thirty-Six

Savage and Harley rode in silence till they got within shouting distance of where the Barefoot clan was camped. The pungent odor of burning wood told Savage they were getting close to the Barefoot camp.

A dozen men and boys lounged around the campfire, talking in low voices, watching the old man they called Daddy pacing back and forth, wearing a path in the prairie sod. His eyes were focused on the two riders approaching from the west.

"Daddy!" Harley called.

With his left hand, Daddy shaded his eyes from the glare of the lowering sun. With his right, he motioned them in. A minute later, Savage and Harley tugged their mounts to a stop in front of the crusty old man with white whiskers.

Savage didn't have to be told that he was face-to-face with Angus Barefoot, the patriarch of the Barefoot clan, who had signed the note. Strutting about, head thrown back, like a peacock preening its feathers. Tough as a boot, and, Savage guessed, stubborn as a corner post.

Harley said, "Daddy, this here is Mr. Will Savage. He has came to talk to you about lettin' Henry go."

Angus glanced with an amused smile at the group around the fire. They snickered as though Harley had just told them a funny story.

Savage was not amused. He searched the shadows for Henry, but didn't see him.

Back and forth beside where Savage sat the mare, Angus moved like a mountain lion planning his attack. Silas had tried to talk him out of it, but Angus was determined to exact retribution. Luke and Wilson were dead, and Savage killed them. What "the partic'lars was" didn't matter

Savage's right hand brushed the revolver strapped to his thigh. He wondered why it was still there, why nobody had tried to take it from him.

He would soon know why.

"You killed my boys," Angus stated, his voice rising in anger. "Us Barefoots don't take kindly to folks killin' our kin."

Wilson had told him the same thing.

In a sudden move, Angus lashed Savage across the shoulders with the riding crop. He swung for a blow to the head, but Savage grabbed the whip, twisted it out of the old man's grasp, and threw it into a brier thicket out of reach.

"I want to see the boy," he demanded.

The men around the campfire scrambled to their feet as if to charge the incensed cowboy, but Angus stopped them with an outstretched arm.

Again Savage said, "I want to see the boy."

Angus's defiant glare told him he was in no mood to negotiate, and dared him to do anything about it.

Savage figured if he could get his gun pointed at the old man without getting himself killed—

In a flash the notion became action. Savage whipped out his gun and leveled it at Angus's head.

A dozen guns from around the fire instantly took aim at Savage where he sat the sorrel mare.

"I see the boy," he said to the clan, "or this thing ends right here."

Angus stood stiff as a poker, glaring at the man with the gun aimed at his head. From somewhere inside, Angus heard a commanding voice say,

"Vengeance is mine, saith the Lord!"

Vengeance for Angus Barefoot would have to wait, however, for an irate cowboy had a Colt's .45 lined up with his eyeballs. Savage was ready to squeeze the trigger and blow Angus all the way to where he could greet the Lord face-to-face. Savage knew his body parts likely would be strewn over the Kansas prairie by the Barefoots' guns, but that wouldn't save Angus.

"Silas!" Angus barked.

Uncle Silas emerged from the shadows, leading Henry by an arm.

Savage took a good look.

"Are you all right, Henry?" he said.

"Yes, sir," Henry said with a shaky voice.

Savage was not satisfied. To Angus, he said, "Let the boy go."

Angus's stubbornness took over. He threw out his chin, and stood his ground.

"You've got me," Savage said. "Let the boy go."

"The boy will be free," Angus said, "when the soil is wet with your blood!"

Silas took Henry's arm and led him away.

"Are they gonna kill you, Will?" Henry cried. "I don't want them to kill you."

Savage holstered his gun, puzzled still as to why he was allowed to keep it.

"Bradley!" Angus shouted.

The puzzle was about to be solved.

From the group around the fire stepped a slender young man of twenty. He was grinning, ready to do the bidding of the grizzly old man he called Daddy.

"This here is Bradley Barefoot," Angus said to Savage. To Bradley, he said, "This is Will Savage, the man who killed your brothers, and the man you're going to kill." Back to Savage, "Bradley is our best shooter. You and him are going to square off out there in the open, man to man."

Bradley leaped onto his horse and sped away to the far end of an open area which Angus designated as the field of battle.

"Harley!" Angus shouted.

Harley guided Savage to the opposite end of the clearing, facing Bradley. He then joined the others on the sideline, eagerly anticipating the action, like spectators at a joust.

Angus pointed a revolver in the air above his head.

"When I fire this pistol," he announced in a loud voice, "you will ride at full gallop toward each other, and fire when ready."

He squeezed the trigger, the shot rang out, and the duel on horseback was underway.

Bradley got a good jump and bore down on Savage's left side. He fired one shot that missed.

Savage held his weapon at the ready but didn't fire, waiting for the right moment.

Reversing course, both men spun their mounts about and raced headlong toward each other. Bradley fired again, and the slug slashed Savage's sleeve. Savage zig-zagged the little mare, wheeled sharply, and fired once.

Bradley pitched backward off his horse and died with a bullet in his heart.

The Barefoots to a man made a move as if to go to Bradley's aid.

The old man yelled, "No!" and they stayed where they were on the sidelines.

With Bradley dead, Savage thought the fight was over. He was wrong.

Two more riders dashed onto the field to face him.

Angus fired the starting shot, and the two Barefoots galloped toward Savage with pistols drawn, one on the right, one on the left. Savage shot the man on the right. The young man grabbed his wounded side but stayed aboard. Savage, hovering low to the mare's neck, shielded himself from the second rider's shots. On the return, Savage finished the injured man with a shot to the head, then ripped a slug into the chest of the other. Both men tumbled off their horses and fell dead.

Again there was anxious movement on the sidelines, and again Angus stopped them with a word.

Savage watched in disbelief as three more young Barefoots rode full tilt onto the field and lined up against him. Angus fired, and the three burst forth, waving their guns, firing wildly, missing their mark.

Savage's little mare worked her heart out, valiantly responding to his commands. Savage drove a slug into the chest of the rider on his left, then felt a violent quiver. The mare was hit. She screamed, her legs stiffened, she leaped and twisted and pawed the air, but she did not give up. Blood spurted from the wound in her head. Finally, her knees buckled, and she crumpled to the ground, and died there.

Savage leaped from the saddle and landed in a heap, struggling to right himself.

The two remaining Barefoot riders were bearing down on him with guns blazing.

From somewhere out of the shadows he heard the crack of a Winchester, and the second Barefoot pitched backward off his horse, and landed on the turf at Savage's feet. He didn't move.

Flat on his stomach, Savage took dead aim at the third Barefoot, squeezed the trigger, and blew him out of the saddle. Anticipating Angus's next move, Savage took cover behind his dead mare. The confused expression of the flint-faced tyrant told Savage that Angus was as surprised as he by the crack of the Winchester.

"Barefoot!" Savage yelled. "Is that it?"

Strangely, Angus shifted his attention from Savage, and signaled his men to concentrate their fire at where the Winchester shots came from. The repeater rifle never let up, finding its mark, even in the half light of the dying day. Within minutes, the only Barefoot left standing was old Angus.

When it was over, smoke hung like fog on the heavy air, and a dozen members of the Barefoot clan, men and boys, lay dead.

Off to his left, Savage searched the shadows for the man with the Winchester, but could see no one.

Pain wracked his left side where the bullet struck. Warm blood matted his shirt near where the bag of gold was still in place. He got to his feet and started walking toward where the wild-eyed old man stood rigid as a flagpole, defiant and confused.

"What about the boy?" Savage said.

Angus's right hand hovered near the gun on his hip. For a long moment he glared at Savage as if he might use it on him. But then Angus waved a hand, and Henry appeared out of the shadows.

Tearfully the boy ran to Savage and clung to him.

"You have destroyed my family!" Angus shrieked.

"There was no call for this, Mr. Barefoot."

"Maybe one day—" Angus sputtered. "Before the Lord takes me—" He stood silent for a time, his eyes riveted on Savage. Then his body relaxed.

In a calm voice, he said, "No harm would have come to the boy. Life is too precious."

Savage shook his head, incredulous.

"I'll need a horse," he said.

With a hopeless gesture toward the horses standing about, Angus said, "They're no good to me now."

Savage loosened the cinch on his saddle and peeled it from the back of the lifeless mare. He then stripped the saddle from a bay and replaced it with his own. He mounted the bay, handed Henry up behind him, and reined toward town.

Angus Barefoot, once proud and defiant, stood beaten and alone, humbled by the reality of defeat by the man he had come to kill.

Thirty-Seven

Were you scared, Will?"

It was a wordless ride to town until Henry broke the silence.

"You bet, Henry."

"Are you gonna be mad at me?"

"No, I"m not mad at you."

"You got your shirt and pants all bloody."

"I've been worse off. Were you scared?"

The boy sniffled, fighting back tears.

"I thought they were gonna kill you," he said.

"They tried."

As the two weary travelers approached Buffalo Flats, blinking lights of the town grew larger and brighter. And Savage thought he knew whose Winchester had saved his life.

At the front gate of Mrs. McClellan's Boarding House, Savage drew rein, and Henry slid off the bay's rump.

News of the clash between Savage and the Barefoots had spread fast.

Meg and Mrs. McClellan burst out the door.

"Will!" Meg shouted. "Are you all right?"

Mrs. McClellan reached for Henry, comforting him with an arm around his shoulders.

"You poor child!" she said.

"I'll take care of him," Meg said, leading Henry away.

She looked back at Savage. He waved at her, then tumbled off his horse.

"Will!" Meg screamed. She rushed to him as he hit the ground. "Help me move him inside. Somebody get a doctor!"

"There's no doctor here, dear," Mrs. McClellan said. "The nearest one is Doc Stark in Dodge City."

"Henry," Meg said, "can you run to the telegraph office and tell them to send a wire to Doctor Stark?"

Henry took off running.

"And tell them to hurry!"

The last thing Savage remembered before he passed out was hearing Meg McGraff say, "We'll put him in here," as she pushed open the door to her room.

Thirty-Eight

Castledine saw the flickering lamplight through Aubrey's cabin window, and braced himself for another unpleasant encounter with his errant brother. He should have known from the beginning that Aubrey was running from something. Why else would he hole up in a rat's nest like that old shack? Castledine was sure of one thing: Aubrey was no damn good.

Just like his old man.

Cliff Roan never put in a full day's work after he married John's mother Nan.

His father, Caleb Castledine, had left his widow well cared for with money from his saddlery in Ellsworth, but Cliff blew it on gambling and booze.

When John was eighteen, he challenged Cliff to account for the money. His mother sided with her husband, and John left home. The only time he went back was for her funeral eight years later. By then Aubrey was already wearing a troublemaker's brand.

At forty-two, Castledine was running out of options. He could bend the rules by which he lived and save his worthless brother, or he could preserve his reputation as an honorable man and respected law enforcement officer, and bring Aubrey to justice. He couldn't have it both ways.

He had already decided which way it was going to be.

He dropped a rein over a sycamore branch and went inside the cabin. Aubrey was lounging on the makeshift bed. The dingy quilts were in a crumpled mass. Empty whiskey bottles and ashes from the pot-bellied stove were strewn over the dirt floor. Food scraps littered the wired-up wooden table.

"Do you ever think about cleaning this place up?" Castledine said.

"Yeah, well, that don't make no difference," Aubrey said, waving a half empty bottle. "Next time you see me, I may be in Denver or Kansas City."

"That's not a bad idea," Castledine said with a flicker of hope that Aubrey would clear out, and the problem of what to do about him would be solved.

"New territory might be good for you."

"Oh, no you don't," Roan blurted. "It ain't that easy. I ain't goin' no place and leave you here with Carrie all to yourself." He swigged at the bottle. With a vicious grin, he said, "Surprised I know about you and that little whore?"

Castledine had no reason to care one way or the other whether Aubrey knew about him and Carrie. Carrie feared for their lives, but he saw no point in pursuing the matter. Aubrey might have been guessing anyway. The surprise was that, if Aubrey did know about him and Carrie, Carrie had told him.

Why would she do that?

"Now, let me tell you something, Aubrey," Castledine said. He was mad, and Roan knew it. "I've moved out of my last town because of some stupid caper of yours. In Hays it was rape, in Shawnee it was card cheating, in North Platte—"

"Aw, common, John! That was a long time ago."

"Not long enough. I've cleaned up after you for the last time!"

"Yeah, well, what about Savage? I don't know if I can handle him by myself."

"You couldn't handle Bo Peep in a gunny sack! And you'd better find a way to keep from coming up against Will Savage, because he'll kill you."

"Well hell, John—"

123

"Savage can't hurt you if he can't find you. If you stay out of sight, and don't make any foolish moves, maybe this will blow over."

His ears echoed with the hollowness of his words. He knew men like Savage. Savage wouldn't quit until he got to Roan. Castledine recognized the dogged determination in his eyes, and the unshakable set of his jaw. Could Castledine head Savage off?

Did he want to?

The marshal stormed out of the shack, mounted the black stallion, and headed back to town. He pondered the toughest problem he ever faced. Its name was Aubrey Roan.

He had an idea that Savage already knew where Aubrey was hiding out.

Thirty-Nine

Doc Stark found Savage unconscious on Meg's featherbed.

Meg had done what she could to make him comfortable: She swabbed his wounds, changed his bandages she made from her bed sheets, and mopped his feverish brow. But Savage didn't know it.

He didn't know anything. All night he had been lucid one minute and unconscious the next.

Doc pointed to a jagged tear on Savage's left side.

"That's where the bullet went in," he said to Meg. He pointed to a spot farther back. "And here is where it came out. He's lucky that slug didn't take up residence in there some place."

He replaced the bandage, then pulled the sheet up to Savage's chin.

"I gave him something to keep him quiet for a while. If he's as tough as I thought when I saw him before, he'll be up and about in no time."

"I'll take care of him," Meg said.

Doc Stark folded his bag and took a step toward the door. A thin smile crossed his lips.

"I kind of thought you might," he said. "A good woman can do more for what ails a man than all the medicine in the world."

Meg walked him to the door.

"He's a very lucky man," Doc said. "So is that boy. Even with all the commotion, maybe it's best that Henry didn't make it to Dodge City after all. He's better off here, with you looking after him."

Doc left, and Meg closed the door.

"Okay, cowboy," she said to the unhearing Savage. "We're getting you over this."

Meg McGraff was born to parents who settled outside Denver back in the fifties. In the winter of her sixteenth birthday, her mother Deborah died of pneumonia. Meg and her father Klee grew closer, drawing strength from each other, nursing the wounds of their loss. Wherever he went, Klee wanted his daughter by his side.

So great was his sorrow, however, that he began drinking heavily. Meg tried to ease his pain, but over time, a bottle of whiskey replaced her as his constant companion. He rejected her efforts to console him, and became violent.

For the first time in her life, Meg was afraid of her father.

"Stay away from me!" he screamed in a drunken rage. He stumbled over a chair. Meg moved to help him. He shoved her aside. "I don't need you! I need my beloved Deborah!"

Meg would never forget the night Klee drained the dregs from a bottle and demanded that she bring him more whiskey.

"There is no more, Papa," she cried.

"Damn you, girl, get me some whiskey!"

"You drank it, Papa. It's all gone."

"Then we'll just by god go get some more."

He grabbed Meg's arm and staggered to the door, dragging her with him. She fought to free herself, but was no match for his farrier's raw-boned strength. Klee forced her, struggling and weeping through wind and snow, all the way to the Red Bull Saloon. He shoved her through the door, then flung her against the bar.

"Whiskey!" he demanded of Charlie Crum, the bartender. "Gimme some whiskey!"

Crum said, "It looks like you've had enough, Klee. I can't sell you any more whiskey."

"Sell hell!" Klee raged. He pushed Meg toward Crum. "What am I bid?"

"Papa, please," Meg pleaded.

"Come on!" Klee screamed, waving his arms at the stunned patrons. "Any of you big tough studs have the price of a bottle of whiskey?"

Nobody moved, and nobody spoke. Everybody stared in disbelief.

"Bid, damn you!" Klee shouted. "She's prime stock. Out of Deborah by old Klee here. What am I bid?"

His bleary-eyed gaze went around the room, scanning solemn faces, questioning, challenging.

"You stinking bastards!" he snorted. "You call yourselves men!"

His foggy eyes came to rest on the somber face of Charlie Crum.

Charlie looked at him as if he were a mischievous child.

"Why don't you go on home, Klee?" he said. "And take Meg with you."

McGraff bristled. "Why you low-life son of a bitch! Who the hell do you think you're talking to?"

"Go on, Klee. We don't want any trouble."

"Trouble? You don't know what trouble is!"

He reached over the bar and grabbed at Crum. Charlie caught his arm and pushed him away. Klee's eyes were slits of hatred. He laid hold of Meg, and shoved her toward the door.

"Wait a minute," Crum said, and Klee stopped. "Why don't you let Meg stay the night here, Klee? I'll ask Molly to look after her."

McGraff stuck out his chin, and said, "If I don't get no bottle, you don't get no Meg."

Crum glanced at Meg. Her body was trembling, her eyes wet.

"All right," he said. "You let Meg stay, and I'll give you a bottle."

"No, papa, please."

"Why, you sniveling little—"

He raised a hand to strike her.

Crum yelled, "Klee!"

Klee dropped his hand.

"Gimme the bottle," he said.

Charlie placed a bottle on the bar.

"This means you go straight home," he said, "and stay there till Meg comes home tomorrow."

"Don't you tell me what to do, Charlie Crum! I'll do what I damn well please!"

Charlie grabbed the bottle to take it away..

Klee swiped his sleeve across his dry mouth. The bottle was slipping away. With a sideways glance at Meg, he said, "Gimme the bottle."

Crum slid the bottle down the bar. Klee snatched it up, and reeled out through the door.

Meg wiped her eyes.

A moment later, the silence was shattered by a scream from outside.

Charlie Crum was the first to get there.

Klee had stumbled off the porch and down the steps. The bottle shattered. A jagged edge was buried in his chest. Blood and alcohol soaked the front of his shirt, and trickled down, making a dark red puddle in the snow.

Klee was dead. His hand was still clutching the neck of the broken bottle.

Forty

Between the sheets of Meg's featherbed, Savage had hardly moved for hours at a time. At other times he tossed and turned, as though fighting to free himself from some unidentified terror. Sometimes he felt the pressure of gentle hands upon him, soft and caressing, bathing his body with cool damp cloths. In his delirium he once heard the frantic voice of a woman crying out to him, calling his name.

From her pallet on the floor beside the bed, Meg kept her vigil through the night. She slept little, often waking to check on him. Trying to make him comfortable.

"Don't worry, Savage," she said in the night, rearranging covers he had kicked off. "You're coming out of this."

Applying bandages to his wounds as Doc Stark instructed, she watched for signs of regained strength.

"Come on, Cowboy," she cooed. "You're not dying in my bed."

When he slept, Meg heard him mumbling words. Most of them she couldn't understand.

One word she heard distinctly was "Carrie."

The morning of the second day, Meg returned from Mrs. McClellan's kitchen with a basin of fresh water to bathe his wounds. She placed the basin on the table beside the bed. Will was staring straight up at her with his eyes wide open.

"Will!" she said.

129

"Howdy, Meg. What're you doing in my room?"

"It's not your room. It's my room."

"Your room?"

"Here," she said. "You have to lie back while I change your bandages."

He did as he was told.

"Doc Stark says you're mighty lucky that bullet came out instead of taking up residence in there some place."

"Doc Stark?"

"He was here yesterday."

"Well, I'll be damned."

"There." She pulled the sheet up to his chin. "That should hold you for a while."

Watching her dispose of soiled bandages, he studied the deep green of her round eyes, the flowing red hair that swirled when she tossed her head. The full lips, the dimple in her left cheek that deepened when she smiled, which was most of the time.

His eyes wandered to the dresser with its oval-shaped mirror suspended between two bowed uprights, and to the chiffonier against the opposite wall.

He noted the white lace curtains framing the double window. Below the window sat a cedar chest. On top of the chest rested an old felt hat with a greasy band. The brim was pressed almost flat, and three bullet holes perforated the crown.

While she folded new bandages Meg watched his gaze settle on the hat.

"I almost replaced that for you," she said.

"You mean—"

"The hat. It's dirty and smelly and has holes in the crown."

"Well, now I know about all that. If it hadn't been for that old hat, those holes might have been in my head."

"You're hopeless, Will Savage. You men feel more strongly about an old hat than you do about your women."

He watched the dimple in her cheek deepen.

"And what about you, Meg?" he wanted to say, but did not. "What is it that you feel strongly about?" Instead, he said only, "So, this is your room?"

"Uh-huh."

"Pretty fancy stuff. Candles, store bought curtains."

"Mrs. McClellan had those stored away. She gave them to me."

"Boy howdy! There was a time when I would have—"

"Who is Carrie?"

Savage was startled by the question. He pinned her with a blue-eyed stare, trying to find in her face what had prompted the question.

"Carrie," he said.

Across his mind flashed a dream he had during one of his unconscious times. In the dream he had heard a voice crying out to him. "Oh, Will! Oh, Will, Will, Will!" He reached for her, but she kept slipping away.

Yes, he knew now, it was Carrie.

"Did I talk?" he said to Meg.

She started to move away, but he caught her hand.

"You need to know about Carrie," he said, "but can I pick the time for telling you?"

She drew her hand from his.

"How long have I been in your room?" he said.

"Since the night before last."

"And Henry? What about Henry?"

"He's all right," was her cool reply. "I took care of him."

"I've been here all this time—and you took care of me too?"

She nodded. "Sometimes you'd wake up and yell at me, then go back to sleep."

"I yelled at you?"

"You didn't know it. You didn't know anything."

He took her hand again.

"You're a good woman, Meg McGraff."

"I know."

He drew her to him. She did not resist.

131

When her father died, Charlie had helped Meg settle in Denver. He gave her a job as a barmaid at the Red Bull, a chance to make her own way.

After a few months, seeking greater opportunity for his two sons, Charlie decided to move his family to Kansas.

Meg was grateful for what Charlie did for her, but thought that a seventeen-year-old girl could better support herself in Denver than in the uncertainty of what she might find in the wide open spaces of Kansas. She stayed behind in Denver when the Crums moved away.

A year later, a fight broke out in the Red Bull Saloon. Some drunken rounder shot holes in the coal oil lamps, and the wooden structure went up in flames. For Meg it was time to move on. She moved from town to town, settling for a time wherever the action was. Mining, timber, ranching, she followed them all, most recently to Hays City, Kansas.

Charlie learned she was in Hays, and sent word, urging her to come help him out at the Last Dog Saloon in Buffalo Flats.

After a warm welcome, Charlie told her, "Molly's gone, Meg."

"I heard, Charlie. I'm sorry."

"And my boys—I sent them back to Denver to get some schooling. I don't hear from them much, but I'm sure they're doing all right."

Meg knew how much Charlie's sons meant to him. She read the hurt in his eyes, and heard the pain in his voice when he talked about them, not hearing from them.

She stroked his cheek with the tips of her fingers, letting him know she understood his hurt.

"I'll never forget what you've done for me," she said. "I hope some day I can pay you back for that."

"You already have," Charlie said. "You came when I needed you."

Forty-One

Meg tucked the sheet under her chin. To Savage, she said, "Now you know what has been happening to me, but you haven't told me why you're in Buffalo Flats."

Will's fingers ran down the front of his shirt, fastening buttons.

He sat on the side of the bed.

"Out around Junction City," he said, "I've got some ground where I graze a herd of cattle. The bad part is, the grazing hasn't been good for sometime because of the drought, and I had to borrow money to keep it going. Now, the banker I borrowed from has decided to call my loan, and I don't have the money to pay it off. If I don't get him a thousand dollars by the first of the month, he can foreclose on me."

"Oh, Will!"

"There's a good side. A man named Aubrey Roan killed a marshal in Abilene a while back. It turns out the marshal—Joe Freeman—had a price on his head from some old charge out west. I'm supposed to find this Roan fellow and give him a reward for killing Freeman."

"A reward? Then what happens to Roan?"

"I asked the judge that same question. He said the Freeman case takes precedence over Roan's."

"So, Roan kills the marshal, and not only gets away with it, but gets paid for it."

"It doesn't make sense, does it? But, it's worth a thousand dollars to me, and that's how much I need to save my cows."

"And this Roan—is he here in Buffalo Flats?"

"I've got a line on him."

He saw no need to burden Meg with the details. She knew neither Roan nor Castledine, and their being brothers would matter little to her.

"You'll find him then?" she said.

"I'll find him."

Meg reached into a drawer of the bedside table and brought out a small leather pouch with a drawstring at the top.

"You'll want to take this with you," she said, holding it out to him. "I found it when I dressed your wounds."

"That's Roan's bag of gold," he said with thanks. "I'm lucky nothing happened to it out there."

"Did the Barefoots have anything to do with that?"

"Not a thing. There was a lot of dying that didn't have to be done." Had it not been for that Winchester, he mused, he might have been one of them.

At the door, he said, "What is today's date?"

"August twenty-first."

Ten days between him and a showdown with Lester Hogan.

"You know, Meg, you haven't changed since the first time I saw you. I still think about that sometimes."

He left, and she said, "So do I."

Remembering, watching Savage close the door behind him, Meg smiled. Embarrassed even now that she had been such a brazen huzzy that time, her face flushed red, and she pulled the covers over her head.

But she was still smiling.

Forty-Two

Carrie grabbed the brown bottle by the neck and emptied it into a glass, seeking refuge in the whiskey to ease the pain, escaping for a while the shambles her life had become. It didn't work. The misery hadn't gone away. Will Savage had, John Castledine had. And Denver Dunn was dead because she enticed Aubrey Roan to kill him.

Why she had allowed herself to get involved with a no-good like Aubrey was a puzzle she would ponder for the rest of her life. Worthless as Dunn was, the guilt of plotting his murder tormented her days, and brought sleepless nights.

It wasn't all her fault, she protested defiantly. She was too young and innocent to suspect Dunn would deceive her about Savage's being killed in that Indian raid. How Dunn managed to have Savage declared dead, she didn't know. What she did know was that she had had no place else to turn.

Life with Will had been so simple. Yes, he was gone a lot, and she spent much time alone. But, they loved each other, and she knew he would come home to her once his job was done.

Why couldn't she have stayed young and vibrant and happy as she was then?

She heard a knock on her door.

"Go away!" she said.

"It's me, Aubrey."

"I know it's you, Aubrey!" she mocked, gulping from the glass.

"Let me in, Carrie." He rattled the doorknob. "I need to talk to you."

"We've got nothing to talk about."

"Damn it, Carrie, let me in!"

"Get away from my door!"

"Carrie!"

"Get the hell away from my door!"

Aubrey banged the door with a fist and stormed away.

Carrie drained the glass and flung it angrily against the door. Flying glass splattered over the room.

She left it where it fell.

Forty-Three

Amos Cully was parked at his favorite poker table in a corner of the Last Dog Saloon. Behind cupped hands he hid his cards from three other players, who were hiding theirs from him. Over the top of his folded hands he saw Meg approaching the table.

"How's Will doing?" he said to her.

"Champing at the bit," Meg said. In the edge of her eye she saw Savage coming through the batwings. "Well, speak of the devil," she said. "Here he comes now."

"Hey you, Meg lady," a thirsty puncher called from a nearby table. "How 'bout a little service over here?"

With a smile and a nod to Savage, she stepped away.

"I'm coming, cowboy," she said. "Don't go working up a sweat."

"Well, lookee here what the cat drug in," Cully said as Savage pulled up beside him.

"I'm mighty glad to see you up and at 'em again, podnah."

"So am I," Savage said. "Can I see you for a minute?"

Amos got up and stepped away from the table. Somebody grumbled, "Don't be long, Cully. I'm still down a passel."

"What is it, Will?" Amos said.

"You told me back in Abilene that I didn't know who my friends were till I needed them real bad.."

"Yeah."

137

"Well, I don't know how many times you can pull me out of a tight spot, but I want to thank you for helping me out against those Barefoots."

"Helpin' you out?" Amos scratched his head.

"With the Winchester. There was no way in hell I would have got out of there alive if you hadn't shown up."

"What Winchester?"

"At the end there, when those two Barefoots were coming at me, and you cut them down with the Winchester."

"Will," Amos said. "I wanted to go out there, but that marshal told me to stay put, and let you handle it your own way." With a hang dog shake of his head, he said, "I should've went anyhow."

"It wasn't you, Amos?"

"I don't own a Winchester, Will. I'm still totin' that old Springfield that I've carried for half my life."

Savage gave that some thought, then said, "There's your skunk in the woodpile again, Amos. If it wasn't you, who could it have been?"

"I don't know who it was, podnah, but I guaran-damn-tee you, you ain't lookin' at 'im."

"Cully!" came a sharp voice from the poker table. "Time's a-wasting!"

Amos ignored him.

"Anything new on Roan?" he said to Savage.

"The first thing tomorrow morning I'm riding out to that shack. I've wasted too much time. I need to wrap this thing up and get back to Junction City."

"Need some help?"

Savage grinned. "You never know."

"I'll see you, Will," Cully said, and stepped back to the poker table.

Savage felt a tug at his elbow. It was Meg.

"Well, look who's here," he said. "Can you visit a minute?"

"A minute is about all. We're busy tonight. Old Charlie Crum will be after me with a hickory stick if I stay too long."

"I know about old Charlie. He'll never change if he lives to be a hundred."

"And he might," she said.

"How's Henry?"

"He's coming around. That was quite an ordeal for him too. Did Henry tell you how it happened?"

"There wasn't much time."

"He told me he left the stage at the way station and started walking, trying to get back to you."

"Back to me?"

"He collapsed in the heat, and the Barefoots came along and picked him up."

"Henry never wanted to go to Dodge."

"That's part of it."

He cast her a questioning look. "What's the other part?"

"He thinks the sun rises and sets in you, Will. He hardly knew his father. Since his mother died, he's attached himself to you."

"Now you're sounding like Doc Stark. Henry doesn't even know me, Meg."

She gave her head a thoughtful nod. "Does anybody?"

"Anybody what?"

"Know you, Will Savage."

"Well, now you know me better than anybody else. How long has it been since the first time we—"

"Uh-oh," she said. With a nod she noted the approach of Charlie Crum. "I've been visiting too long."

Charlie said, "You know, I really hate to bust up this cozy little confab." His handlebar mustache twitched when he grinned. "But there's other folks over there that need to be done something for."

"The hell you say, boss man," Meg chided.

"Now, Meg, don't gimme no sass. You can flirt with this feller after I'm gone."

She patted him on the cheek as she left.

"When is that going to be, Charlie?" Savage said.

"Hell, Will, I don't know. It don't make no difference how hard I try, old age just keeps creeping up on me. But, one of these days I'm gonna set fire to this place and head back to Denver where my boys are, and let them take care of me for a change."

Savage wished he had a dollar for every time he'd heard that story. It had been eleven years since Charlie sent his boys back to school in Denver.

He hadn't heard from them since. Retelling the story was Charlie's way of keeping alive the dream of seeing them again.

"Hell's fire, Will, why shouldn't I? I taken care of them all those years after their mama died, and—"

His voice trailed off as he turned away.

"Charlie," Savage said.

Charlie paused. He waited a couple of seconds before facing his friend. The tone of Will's voice, and the look on his face, told Charlie the time he hoped would never come had come.

"Yeah, Will?"

"You remember my wife—Carrie?"

"Sure, Will." Charlie swallowed hard. "I remember."

"I thought you might have seen her, or heard something about where she might be."

Charlie moved a step closer, watching Will watching him. Using the moment to search for an answer that might satisfy his friend. No, he hadn't seen Carrie, but he knew where she was. Carrie was upstairs in room 203.

Jimmy had checked her in. She hardly left her room, except for an occasional ride. She even took her meals up there. Her first and only visitor after she moved in was Marshal John Castledine. Until lately. Some younger fellow had been seen going in and out of room 203.

Out of respect for Will, Charlie hadn't paid Carrie a call.

"Will," Charlie said, "you know Carrie married that Dunn feller after they said you died in that Sioux raid."

"I heard about that."

"Then somebody said Dunn got shot up in a poker game over at Dodge."

Charlie fell silent. He wished the floor would open up and swallow him whole, so he wouldn't have to tell his friend that Carrie was sharing her bed with the town marshal?

Savage knew when Charlie wasn't talking there was something he didn't want to tell.

"Charlie?" he said.

"Will, I got to tell you—"

"What about Carrie, Charlie?"

Charlie balked as long as he could. Much as it hurt, he couldn't lie to him. Get it out, and get it over with. He spread his hands in a gesture of helplessness. Will would keep pushing till he squeezed the truth out of him.

He had to know sometime.

With a jerk of his head toward the stairway across the room, Charlie blurted, "Upstairs in room 203."

Savage was afraid to believe what he thought he heard Charlie say. "You mean she's here—at the Last Dog?"

"I wanted to tell you, Will, but— I guess I didn't really want you to know because—"

Charlie was eager to be gone. "By the way, Will," he said, moving away. "The marshal said if I saw you—he needs to talk to you."

Savage needed to talk to the marshal too. Stunned as he was by Charlie's news about Carrie, though, he struggled whether to go looking for Castledine—or Carrie.

For a long time Savage pondered whether he should mount the stairs and find room 203. He questioned whether Carrie would care to see him. After four years of wondering, he still needed to see her to find out— What was it he needed to find out?

Suddenly he was on his feet, mounting the steps. At the door marked 203, he lifted a fist, and gave the door a sharp rap. There was no answer. Disappointed, he almost turned away, then decided to try once more.

A harsh voice from the other side of the door yelled, "I told you I've got nothing to say to you. Now get the hell away from my door, and stay away!"

Savage gulped.

"Carrie, it's Will," he said. "Will Savage."

The door opened a crack, and Carrie peeked through it. Her hair was disheveled, eyes brooding. In a long white robe, she glared up at him.

"What the hell are you doing here?" she scowled, stepping aside to let him in. "I thought we settled up four years ago."

"I heard you were in town."

"Who told you that?"

"Charlie. Charlie told me."

"Charlie would! I haven't seen hide nor hair of him since I got here. He always was on your side!"

Savage stared at the woman who once was his wife. The woman he'd longed to see and hold and love as he had before. But, no longer was she the soft, sensitive girl he married twelve years ago. Gone was the sweet innocence that drew him to her the first time he saw her at Blanchard's back in Abilene. She was still beautiful, but with a harshness he had never seen.

"I heard about Denver," he said.

"That son of a bitch!" she roared. "That low-life son of a bitch!"

"Charlie said you had a son."

"Hah! That's all I ever got from Denver Dunn. A son! Born blind and crippled. Denver never cared about him, and I never wanted him. An imbecile— just like his old man. Was I supposed to saddle myself with that garbage for the rest of my life?"

Like a bull in a chute she raged, paced back and forth across the room, rarely looking at Savage, spewing venom, blaming everybody and everything, except herself for her miserable plight.

Savage was not comfortable.

"I think I'd better go," he said.

"Just a minute."

She stepped to the bureau, opened a drawer, and brought out a small music box. Savage recognized it as the first present he ever gave her.

"You gave me this once," Carrie said, "a long time ago. I thought you might want it back."

She tossed the music box to him. He grabbed at it, but it dropped short, and shattered on the floor.

"What the hell?" she said. "I never liked it anyway."

"Goodbye, Carrie."

Savage hesitated outside her door. He didn't want it to end this way. Yet, she had let him know there was nothing left over from before, and whatever he felt for her would fade in time.

The shattered music box had closed the door on the past, and it was time to move on.

With an ear to the door, Carrie listened as the sound of Will's footsteps died away down the hall. She wanted to call him back, but gave him no reason to care if he ever saw her again. She collapsed on her featherbed and sobbed into a pillow. Hating the wreckage she had made of her life, she regretted not seeking Will out as soon as she learned he was in Buffalo Flats.

But then, what would she have done about Marshal John Castledine?

And what now would become of the guileless young girl who so long ago sold Will Savage a suit of winter underwear?

Forty-Four

Sometime in the night Savage was jarred awake by a heavy-fisted knock on his door.

"Who is it?" he said.

"Messenger," said a gruff voice from the hallway.

"Where from?"

"Abilene. Said it was urgent."

"Give me a minute."

"Hurry it up. We ain't got all night."

More than one man out there. Messengers usually rode alone.

Savage pulled on his clothes, then reached for the revolver in the gun belt slung over the bed post. He eased over to the swing side of the door where the light from the hall wouldn't fall on him when he opened it. Quietly he slipped the bolt on the door.

"All right," he said. "Come on in."

The door flew open, and a volley of lead plunged into the empty bed.

Savage returned the fire, and two men fell dead in the doorway. He toed the bodies over and wondered if they were the same two Amos scared off on the trail. One of them was about forty years old. Savage had seen him hanging around Lester Hogan's bank. The other one was no more than eighteen.

From his window Savage took a look down the street. The light in the marshal's office was still burning. By the time he got downstairs on his way to see Castledine, the marshal was already in the middle of the street in a half run. He had heard the shots and was headed that way.

"Castledine."

"Is that you, Savage? What's going on?"

"A couple of bushwhackers jumped me in my room. I shot them."

"You shot them," the marshal said. Savage's shooting somebody was no longer news. Castledine never broke stride.

"Let's go take a look," he said.

"They're dead."

Outside Savage's room they were greeted by a cluster of curious onlookers. Amos, Meg, and Mrs. McClellan were among them, along with an assortment of drummers and cattle buyers. They were all agape and aghast, wondering what took place in the upstairs room of the tall cowboy.

Mrs. McClellan covered her mouth to stifle a scream.

Castledine assured them that the situation was under control, and sent them all trooping back to bed. Satisfied that dead men don't fire two shots apiece into an empty bed, he called for help and deposited the bodies at Hezzy Thorne's funeral parlor. Hezzy reacted with a perplexed look on his face, as he often did when strange bodies showed up on his preparation table. He appreciated the rash of business lately— except for Mrs. Wadsworth, rest her soul—but he hated being rousted out of a deep sleep to take care of it.

When Castledine escorted the bodies in, Hezzy displayed a tinge of irritation, which was rare for him, especially in the presence of the marshal. Having used up all his burying boxes, Hezzy complained that he would have to wait until Marvin Cribbs could build some more.

"Well then, Mr. Thorne," the marshal said testily, "why don't you just do that?"

Hezzy gave the marshal a saucer-eyed blink, unused to seeing Castledine show any sign of aggravation about anything. He threw up his hands as if to ward of a blow.

Castledine left the funeral parlor, and spotted Savage on the street.

Savage said, "Crum said you wanted to see me."

"I do."

Savage fell in beside him and together they strode down the middle of the street to the marshal's office.

"I hope we never have to meet here, Savage."

Savage didn't have to ask what the marshal meant, but he did anyway.

"Where?"

"In this street."

"Are you aiming to face me down, marshal?"

"If I have to."

Castledine palmed open his office door and walked in ahead of Savage.

He tossed his hat on the desk, and motioned Savage to a chair. Savage stood. Castledine settled into the chair behind his desk.

"You're the one to decide that," Castledine said.

"How's that?"

"You could ride out of here and nobody would know the difference."

At another time, Savage would have challenged him with, "Why would you want me to ride out?" But he already knew the answer. He thought the marshal was grasping at straws in the wind, looking for answers of his own. Some way to save his brother without sacrificing his credibility as a lawman.

"You would know," Savage said. "I would know. And some fellow named Aubrey Roan would know."

Though Castledine had clouded the trail between him and Roan, Savage respected the marshal as a man and lawman. He didn't blame him for wanting to save his brother from a showdown with Savage that Castledine believed Roan wouldn't survive. On the other hand, the marshal's job was to

146

enforce the law, no matter who was involved. Working both sides of his badge, Savage figured, he weighed one side against the other.

Castledine poured himself a cup of hours old coffee, and invited Savage to join him.

Savage shook his head no.

"Some folks are uneasy about having you around, Savage."

What people thought about his being around mattered to Savage about as much as the stale coffee that filled the marshal's cup.

"Is that so?" he said.

"The mayor and his brood would like to see something done about you."

"Like what?"

"They think I ought to lock you up, or run you out of town."

"Uh-huh." Savage spent no time worrying about the mayor and his brood. "What about you, Castledine? Do you want me gone too?"

"Life was a lot less complicated before you showed up. So far you've done nothing I can charge you with. If you had, you'd be cooling your heels in my jail. But you're right on the edge."

"Well, I'll tell you what, marshal, I don't like this town any better than it likes me. I came to where the trail led me. As soon as I get what I came for, I'll be gone. Then you can go to hell, and take your town with you."

"What are you after, Savage?"

"You know damn well what I'm after. To deliver a reward to Aubrey Roan for killing Joe Freeman."

"That's not easy to swallow."

"Swallow what tastes good to you, Castledine. I thought you'd help me locate Roan, and I'd be out of here long before this, but I was wrong about that." He made a move toward the door. "All you've helped me do so far is waste a lot of time."

Castledine stopped him with a question.

"What do you know about this Roan fellow?"

"Not much. He's around thirty years old. Pretty much of a hot head."

Savage thought he must be loco, describing what the marshal's brother was like. Why not just blurt it out and get it done? Sure, you respect him. But why keep playing these silly little games, trying to salvage the marshal's pride, waiting for him to tell you what you already know?

"I hear he flies off the handle without much coaxing," Savage said.

That was Aubrey all right. Castledine lit a cigar, and offered Savage one.

Savage said no. Cigars before breakfast made him sick to his stomach.

The marshal puffed leisurely, exhaling a cloud of gray smoke.

Savage was eager to be gone. He had a job to do. He turned to go and caught sight of a rifle leaning against the wall behind Castledine. He recognized it as a Winchester '73 repeater rifle, like the one he had heard somebody firing against the Barefoots.

A puzzling thought crossed his mind.

"Word gets in and out," Castledine said. "From time to time I get fliers telling me who's wanted." He drained his cup. "If I get anything on Roan, I'll let you know."

"Uh-huh." Savage grunted. That coffee would freeze in Castledine's belly before he heard from him. "You do that."

"What about those two men you shot at the boarding house a while ago? Why would they be coming after you?"

"My guess is they were after the reward money."

"You carry it with you?"

"Yes."

The marshal puffed and blew. Thinking.

"Why don't you leave it with me?" he said. "If I run across that Roan fellow, I'll—"

Savage shook his head. "My deal is to hand it to him myself."

"How many men have you killed, Savage?"

Sarah Wadsworth asked him that same question. He had no answer for her either.

"How long have you been a lawman, Castledine?"

"Seventeen years."

"Do you remember every man you killed?"

"I get paid to kill or not kill," Castledine shot back. "You seem to make sport of it."

"You've got it wrong, marshal. I've faced a lot of men, but—"

"Dead men."

"All but me!"

Savage shoved the door open.

"Savage!"

Savage spun around. The marshal was on his feet, leaning heavily on the desk. His face was drained of color. Savage thought he knew what was coming.

"Aubrey Roan is my brother," the marshal said.

Savage took a step back into the room.

"I know that," he said. It couldn't have been easy for Castledine to admit that. "A friend of mine heard you and Aubrey talking. He told me."

"Cully?" The marshal's voice was tinged with suspicion.

"No, it wasn't Amos."

Castledine's eyes narrowed, doubting the answer.

"I know where Aubrey is," Savage said. "I'm on a short leash to get this done. It would have saved a lot of time if you'd told me this in the beginning."

Castledine threw out his chest.

"Now you know what you're up against," he said.

"You still don't believe there's a reward, do you?"

"I knew Joe Freeman. And I know my brother. If Joe had had any chance at all, Aubrey would be dead, not Freeman." He stretched to his full six-foot five, and looked Savage squarely in the eye. "My brother killed Joe Freeman in a hotheaded fury, Savage. And you expect me to believe he deserves a reward for that?"

"Well, there was that charge against Freeman."

"Stay away from my brother, Savage! I'm the law here. I'll handle this my own way and in my own time."

"I can't do that, and you know it."

Savage left the marshal staring at the door and headed for the livery stable. Whatever he thought of Castledine, he knew he might be facing two men instead of one if it came to that. Either way, it was time he got face to face with Aubrey Roan.

Forty-Five

The first rays of daylight shimmered across the dry prairie and flooded the low-lying hills, pushing the shadows from the deserted street of Buffalo Flats.

Savage reached the livery stable, saddled the bay, and climbed aboard.

The first of the month was closing in, and he had lost too much time because of Henry, Sarah Wadsworth, and the Barefoots. He had to settle with Roan, and get back to Junction City and head off Hogan's foreclosing on him. He was satisfied that the two yahoos he shot at the boarding house were Hogan's men, trying to make sure he didn't collect the thousand dollars and make it back in time to pay off his debt.

He would take care of Hogan, but first he had to deal with Aubrey Roan.

Rounding the back of the Last Dog Saloon, Savage spotted a horse tethered to the rail. A big roan stallion. "As slick and purty a roan stallion as ever I seed," Cap'n Billy had said. Standing right there in plain sight, silhouetted against the light of dawn, whickering softly, as though greeting a friend.

Savage's heartbeat quickened. If Roan was in town, that would save him a ride out to his shack.

The thought was shattered by the clatter of hurried footsteps down the stairs leading to the Last Dog rooms. Savage kneed the bay into the shadows where he could see

151

without being seen. He saw a man make a frenzied dash to where the roan stallion was tied.

"Aubrey Roan," Savage assured himself.

It was Roan all right. Sandy hair, stocky build, about thirty years old. And there was no mistaking that roan stallion.

The front of Roan's shirt was splattered with dark stains, like dirty hand prints.

Roan was in a hurry. He leaped into the saddle, and spurred the roan south on the dead run.

Savage's instincts told him to give chase before Roan made it out of town. But, at that moment, he caught sight of an open door at the top of the stairs. A flickering sliver of light through the doorway struck him with a sudden urgency to know why Roan had dashed away in such a hurry.

Savage dropped rein over the rail near where the roan had stood. He climbed two steps at a time toward the flickering light. He knew where to find Roan when he was ready. Now he needed to find out why he had dirty hand prints on his shirt.

He eased open the door at the top of the stairs and stepped inside. It took a moment for his eyes to adjust to the dimly lit hallway. From an open door he saw a splotch of dancing lamplight on the hallway floor. Was it room 203?

He took a few cautious steps that way. It was 203.

Through the open door he saw a woman crumpled on the floor. Battered and bloody. Her white lace coverlet was soaked with blood.

Could it be—

Savage fell on his knees beside her.

Forty-Six

Aubrey buried a spur in the big stallion's flank. He glanced over his shoulder to be sure he wasn't followed. Seeing no one, he breathed easier, and urged the stallion faster.

"Dumb little bitch!" he muttered. Whoring around with half the men in town, including his own brother! Who the hell did she think she was messing with? Some dim-witted cowpoke with no brains and no pride? Hah! He showed her, he did.

He jerked the reins, and the big horse's legs stiffened, and his hooves dug into the dry prairie sod beside the shack. Roan bounded off and hit the ground running. He was half way to the door before the stallion skidded to a stop.

"I'll get my rifle and a pocketful of shells," he muttered, "and I'll be ready. Brother or no brother, anybody that comes after me gets it in the gut. John had just better sit back there in his cozy little jail house and shine up his badge and play it safe."

It was time Aubrey Roan showed the world what he was made of. He scrounged through the rubble searching for his rifle.

"Make fun of me, would she? Compare me to my big brother, would she?

153

Whorin' little bitch. And that Savage bastard! Who the hell does he think he is—snoopin' around like he was God a'mighty himself? Worse than John.

"Hell yes, I killed Joe Freeman! He never had a chance. I knew he'd be comin' and waited for him. Damn right! Never knew what hit him, old Joe didn't. I killed Denver Dunn too. And Carrie too!"

Aubrey whimpered when he thought of Carrie. He hadn't meant to kill her. But, in a jealous rage he had lost control.

"I killed Carrie," he sobbed, stumbling over the rifle. He covered his face with both hands, and said it again. "I killed Carrie."

He had tried to explain to her that he only came to collect what he thought was coming to him for killing Dunn. Carrie thought differently, and beat off his groping hands.

"You'll collect nothing!" she spat. "You've had all you're going to get!"

"I ain't had nothin'!"

"What does that tell you, Aubrey?"

He grabbed her by the shoulders and pulled her to him in a rage.

"It tells me that if I was my brother, you'd have been spraddle-legged flat on your back before he left the jail!"

She struggled to free herself.

"Your brother is a man!" she said hotly.

"Hah! You think I ain't a man?"

He struck her across the mouth and knocked her to the floor. He kept hitting her and kicking her in a blue-veined rage. He beat her until she quit fighting. She never screamed, nor cried out.

Carrie was dead.

For how long he pounded her lifeless body Aubrey had no notion. Nor how many times he struck her battered face for which he had sacrificed his soul. He was bent on destroying that face, and the body that his arms had ached to hold.

His rage began to fade, and he faced the reality of the foul deed he had committed.

He knelt beside the unmoving body. He cradled her head in his arms. Grieving, crying real tears, crazily caressing her blood-spattered face as if to revive it from its deadness.

Then, in a heartbeat, Roan's grief had given way to panic. His first frantic thought was, "Gotta get out of here! Somebody will find her. They'll be comin' after me! John? No. He wouldn't come after his own brother. Savage?

Savage might come. But why would he care about a woman he never heard of?

Downstairs in the barroom——what if they——"

He threw open the door to room 203 and burst into the hallway. Frantic to get away, he hadn't bothered to close the door. He clattered down the stairs. Hurry! No telling who might be around. Leap onto that big old stallion and get the hell outa here!

He stumbled over the rifle in the rubble, and checked to be sure it was loaded. He then settled into the far corner of the shack, and waited.

Forty-Seven

"**C**ARRIE!"

Savage's whispered cry pushed itself from horrified lips.

Gently he touched the face that once was beautiful and innocent.

He drew the blood stained coverlet close around her body, and lifted it into his arms. Through the door he carried it down the four steps and across the barroom to the batwing doors. Never once did he doubt that the stains on Aubrey Roan's shirt were made by the blood of his beloved Carrie.

He vowed that the sun would not set before Roan paid for that.

It was long past midnight when Charlie Crum fell into bed and had trouble getting to sleep. He finally dropped off an hour before daylight. Then, he was jolted awake by what sounded like some likkered up cowboy shooting up the town.

He couldn't get back to sleep, so he pulled on his clothes, and shuffled back downstairs. He put on a pot of coffee. While it brewed, he grabbed a big white towel and began wiping alcohol drippings off the bar from the night before. He muttered about careless punchers wasting good whiskey.

Across the room from where Charlie wiped and grumbled were the steps leading up to the rooms. Knuckling cobwebs from his eyes, he wouldn't have bet his life savings that what he saw was what he thought he saw. His bleary, sleepless eyes were asking him to believe he saw a tall cowboy carrying down the steps and across his barroom floor a limp lady in a white coverlet splashed with red. The cowboy set a steady course to the batwings, looking neither right nor left.

Charlie rubbed his eyes, hoping for a clearer view. He wished he had his glasses from upstairs.

"Savage?" he said.

The cowboy didn't answer. He kept walking till he got to the batwings and backed his way out, protecting his burden.

Charlie came around from behind the bar, and watched with curious concern as the cowboy descended the wooden steps out front. He carried the woman down the street to Hezzy Thorne's funeral parlor, and disappeared into Hezzy's front door.

"Savage!" Charlie shouted, recognizing his friend in the sunlight. "Carrie!"

Forty-Eight

Hezzy Thorne scratched his balding head and eyed the bodies of the two uglies the marshal had deposited on his preparation table.

The marshal didn't tell him who they were, and there was nothing on their bodies to identify them. To Hezzy they looked like what the dime novels portrayed as "ruffians, brigands, and highwaymen." Long hair, stubbled beards, shifty eyes—if their eyes could have shifted. But, then, Hezzy conceded, most of the carcasses he had laid to rest in the last thirty-three years hadn't looked much different from these two.

Roused out of a deep sleep by the marshal's pounding on his door, Hezzy allowed as how he might as well go to work on them.

He hadn't had so many bodies to work on at one time since the cattle wars. He had buried Luke and Wilson Barefoot, Frank and Curly, and Mrs. Wadsworth, rest her soul. And now these two. He busied himself at the table, thinking that if he had been responsible for burying the rest of those Barefoots—as he heard old Angus had somehow done—he could take the vacation that his wife Mavis had harped at him about for years.

"When are we going to take that trip to St. Louis that you promised me?" She had pestered him for longer than he cared to remember. Usually it was at breakfast when he was struggling to choke down a plateful of her rubbery pancakes that she had placed in front of him every morning of their thirty-seven years together. The kids used to complain, "Pancakes again?" then she'd serve them bland oatmeal till they begged for a return to the rubbery pancakes.

"Hell, woman, I don't know," was Hezzy's standard response to her persistent nagging. "When folks quit dying, I reckon."

That was the point at which Hezzy had arrived in his reflection when his door burst open. He watched with eyes agog as some strange cowboy placed upon his table another body. It was wrapped in a white lace coverlet smeared with blood. The face was battered, the yellow hair matted, lips swollen and bloody.

With a puzzled look, Hezzy said to a cowboy he'd never seen, "What the hell is going on around here?"

The cowboy said, "Carrie. I'll be back."

Hezzy stood with his mouth open and watched him march out of his funeral parlor without a backward glance.

Will Savage was hell-bent for the office of Marshal John Castledine.

The shooting at the boarding house, transferring the bodies to Hezzy's funeral parlor, and his confrontation with Savage had kept Castledine busier than usual in the early morning. In his two years as marshal of Buffalo Flats he had never before been rousted out of bed before sunrise. So now here he was cleaning the Winchester on his desk, pondering the problem of his brother, and what to do about Will Savage.

His door burst open, and he jerked his head up. Filling his doorway were six-feet-four inches of incensed cowboy.

Castledine bounced to his feet, and faced the glaring Savage.

"Your brother!" Savage said.

"My brother?"

"He just killed a woman at the Last Dog rooms. Her name is Carrie."

"Carrie?" The marshal swallowed hard. "Aubrey killed Carrie?"

"I was on my way to settle with him when I saw him run down the back stairs and head south. His shirt was covered with blood."

The marshal stood stiff as a dart, pressing his fingertips against the desk top.

"How do you know it was Carrie?" he said.

Savage took a step closer, staring into his face.

"I ought to know my own wife. Carrie and I used to be married."

Only slightly did the marshal's big body sway.

"I found her on the floor of room 203," Savage said. "She was dead. Beaten to death by that little brother of yours that you've been trying so hard to keep me away from."

"But, if Aubrey—"

"He killed her, Castledine." Savage headed for the door. "And I'm going after him."

"That's what you've wanted all along, isn't it, Savage? To kill him in a shootout so you could collect that reward."

"I've already got the reward, Castledine," Savage said calmly. "All I had to do was deliver half of it to Roan. But the rules have changed now. When Roan killed Carrie, he killed a part of me too." He turned on a heel. "I'm wasting time."

"Savage!"

Savage whirled around. Castledine was standing with his feet spread apart, his right hand hovering near his gun.

Savage waited.

"You get Aubrey," the marshal said in a hoarse whisper, "and you'd better be ready to get me too."

"I'll get him."

"Face me now or face me later!"

"That's up to you." Savage started moving away. "I'll take my chances."

He opened the door, then paused. There was something he needed to do. But what if it hadn't been Castledine? Then he had nothing to lose.

Castledine was still standing bedrock stiff.

Savage said, "I want to thank you for helping me out against those Barefoots."

With a nod, he indicated the Winchester on the marshal's desk. "A Winchester can give a man an edge."

"Go to hell, Savage."

Amos hailed Savage on his way to the livery to pick up his horse.

"There's a lot of talk about what took place at the boardin' house a while ago," Amos said, falling in step beside him. "You reckon them fellers was after the reward money?"

"That's what I think." Savage never broke stride. "I figure Hogan sent them to keep me from getting back there with the loan payment."

In a half trot to keep astride, Amos said, "You in a hurry, Will?"

"Aubrey Roan killed somebody else. I'm going after him. I'll tell you about it later. Keep an eye on that marshal for me. He's Roan's brother, and things could get out of hand."

"His brother? Be damned, Will!"

"I'm betting Roan thinks nobody knows about Carrie, but when he sees me coming, he'll likely head back here, looking for help from Castledine."

"Carrie?"

"That's something else I'll tell you about when there's time."

Savage leaped into the saddle and put a spur to the bay's flank.

"Amos, will you tell Meg what's going on?"

"Sure, Will." Amos scratched his head. What was it he was supposed to tell Meg?

Savage spurred the bay south

Forty-Nine

Savage paused on the knob hill and peered down at Roan's shack, and dragged a sweat-soaked sleeve across his brow. Early though it was, the muggy closeness already caused his shirt to cling to him like a bat to a cave wall.

He angled off across a swale, giving the shack a wide berth. To keep from spooking Roan into taking off, he circled around and came up on the back side of the cabin below the sycamores. He dropped rein, and left the bay to nibble at the grass.

The roan stallion was tethered to a post. Savage put out his hand, steadying the horse so he made no sound that might alert Aubrey in the shack.

Savage pressed his body against the off side of the shack and inched his way to an open window on the west wall. He removed his hat, and sneaked a peek over the window sill. He didn't see Roan. All he could see were empty food cans, discarded whiskey bottles, and ashes from the wood-burning stove strewn over the floor.

Even so, he knew Roan was in there or his horse wouldn't be tied out back.

Savage ducked under the window and moved around to the front of the house, facing the front door.

"Roan," he called. "Aubrey Roan."

"Who is it?"

"Will Savage."

It took a minute for Roan to answer.

"I don't know no Will Savage."

"I need to talk to you."

The door was the only opening at the front of the shack, so, if Roan tried to pull down on him, Savage knew it would be from there.

Savage planted his feet apart, his right hand resting on the butt of his gun.

"So talk!" came the sharp voice from inside.

"Do you want to come out, or do you want me to come in?"

Savage waited.

Slowly the door squeaked half open. In it stood a husky man of medium height, fair complexion, and a growth of beard His eyes never rested.

His right hand was hidden behind the door frame. Savage guessed it was wrapped around a gun butt.

"You want to talk about Joe Freeman," Roan said.

"Partly."

"What else?"

"Denver Dunn."

"Why do you want to talk about Denver?"

"I understand you killed him."

"Who told you that?"

"Word gets around."

"Yeah, I killed old Denver. He wasn't no good for nothin'. Carrie—that's Denver's wife—she wanted him dead."

Savage fought the urge to shatter Roan's insolent mouth with a slug from his .45.

"Fair fight though," Roan said. "Denver drawed first."

"Uh-huh. You've been talking to your brother—about Joe Freeman."

"Brother?" Aubrey's eyes narrowed with suspicion. "I got no brother."

"John Castledine."

"How the hell did— You say your name's Savage?"

"That's right. I've been hoping I'd run into you. I've got a reward for you—for killing Freeman."

"A reward?" Roan had trouble believing that. "John never said nothin' about no reward."

"A thousand dollars."

"A thousand dollars! Just for killin' old Joe?"

"I'm thinking about not giving it to you."

"Not givin' it to me? I got it comin', ain't I? I'm the one that done it."

"Oh, you done it all right," Savage said, seething inside. "I aim to see that you get everything that's coming to you."

In his eagerness to claim the reward, Roan stepped out from the protection of the door jamb, and held out a hand.

"Well, come on," he said. "Gimme the money."

"We've got a little more business to attend to first."

"Yeah? What's that?"

"I'm looking for the man that beat Carrie Dunn to death."

He looked Roan dead in his restless eyes. "Carrie Savage Dunn."

Carrie Savage Dunn?

Roan took a long time deciding his next move. This man—Will Savage. John hadn't told him about Savage and Carrie. Was he a brother to Carrie? How come they had the same name? Maybe her husband? Carrie never said nothin' about a husband besides Dunn.

Either way, there he stood. The man John warned him to steer clear of. A man named Savage, facing him down, his hand hovering close to his gun.

Roan had a fleeting notion to take his chances with Savage. But he wasn't ready for that. He'd have to work up to it. He wasn't sure he could outdraw the man glaring at him, daring him to make a move.

Roan started easing back toward the open door.

"Well now," he said, dropping his head in a diverting motion, "we might have to talk about that."

He made a sudden dash into the shack, and banged the door shut behind him.

Savage took out after him. He shouldered the door open and saw Roan disappear out the window. The sound of pounding hoof beats told him the big stallion was already thundering toward town.

He leaped into the saddle, and spurred the bay toward Buffalo Flats. If Roan got there first, Savage knew he likely would be facing two guns instead of one.

Fifty

Saturday morning was busy in Buffalo Flats. It bustled with cattlemen and farmers at the Mercantile, the bank, the smithy's, or the barber shop. Trading stories, catching up on what happened to cattle prices.

Much of the conversation centered around the stranger's battle with the Barefoots, and his shooting the two bushwhacker's that morning. Some idly speculated as to who might be his next victim.

Edgar Mills brought a laugh at Ross Pickle's barbershop when he joshed the half dozen men waiting on the benches.

"Well, I wouldn't mind if it was Chet Whisenant here," Mills said. "That rascal has cleaned my plow at checkers since grade school."

Whisenant said, "It looks to me like I better be looking over my shoulder to see who's coming up behind me."

The ladies did their household shopping, and shared a cup of flavored tea in Mrs. McClellan's parlor. And, of course, their hostess always favored them on Saturday morning with a special treat fresh from her oven.

While their parents were occupied elsewhere, the youngsters ran free, in and out of alleyways, with barking dogs nipping at their heels, enjoying a romp with their friends.

Wagons of all sizes creaked into town and out again, most of them loaded both ways, trading one load for another, such as grain for a month's provisions. Wagon teams and tethered horses lined both sides of the street.

The arrival of the Overland stage was always anticipated with excitement because one never knew what newcomer or famous lawman might be aboard.

Many recalled the time in the summer of '76 when Wild Bill Hickock spent a night at Mrs. McClellan's Boarding House on his way to Dakota Territory.

Thirteen days later Jack McCall shot him dead with a bullet in the back of his head.

Will Savage walked his bay down the middle of Main Street, scanning both sides for sight of Aubrey Roan. He spotted him just as Orlie Potts wheeled the stage around the corner of the Mercantile.

Roan rolled off his horse in front of the Last Dog Saloon. He flipped a rein over the hitch rail and bounded up the steps to the board walk.

"Roan!" Savage called.

The tone of his voice told all within earshot that Roan was in trouble.

Roan knew it too. His first impulse was to run. But there was Savage facing him, and his horse was too far away to get to safely.

Breathless onlookers skittered aside, anticipating trouble, clearing a path between two angry men they'd never seen before.

"It's that Savage fellow," a man whispered to his neighbor. He was the hawk-faced one who had led Luke Barefoot's horse away with Luke's body on it.

Roan had no place to run. His restless eyes searched the crowd for his brother, but Castledine was nowhere in sight. Roan's shifty eyes landed on a stubby little red-bearded man standing to the right of where Savage sat his bay. He was staring at Roan with an eagle eye. Roan had seen him before, but he couldn't recall where. Maybe Abilene? He wondered if he was in cahoots with Savage.

Savage dismounted, his gaze trained on Roan. He adjusted his gun belt.

Roan shifted his holster to the front of his thigh. He told himself it was time he did something about Savage. He stepped down off the plank walk and onto the street, showing more grit than he knew he had. He was sure his brother would show up in time to save him from the wrath of the stone-faced Savage.

"What do you want, Savage?" Roan said with a smirk. "You want me to say it in front of all these people? I killed Joe Freeman!"

The spectators shook their heads shamefully and fell away.

"Old Joe never had a chance," Roan bragged. "What else do you want, Savage?"

"What about Denver Dunn?"

"Yeah, I told you I killed Dunn. Carrie wanted me to, so I did."

"And Carrie too?"

"Yeah, I killed Carrie." He went for his gun. "And now I'm gonna kill you!"

Savage's gun was a split second away from killing Aubrey Roan when he heard a voice in the crowd.

"Aubrey!"

Roan heard it too. He froze in his tracks, his gun hand in mid-air. He had heard that voice all his life. It belonged to his brother, John Castledine.

"Drop the gun and turn around with your hands up," Castledine ordered.

Aubrey was afraid now that John might shoot him. He hadn't thought so before, but now he wasn't sure. His own brother! Would he do it? Castledine behind him and Savage in front of him. Beads of sweat blistered his row. His palms were clammy.

"Aubrey!" Castledine said. "For once in your life act like a man!"

Roan whirled and fired. The shot went wild. His gun went flying, and plopped to the ground like a bird killed in flight. In the dust of the street, Aubrey Roan lay dead with a slug in his chest, felled by his brother.

Castledine holstered his gun.

Savage did the same, watching the big marshal, anticipating his next move.

Castledine's right hand hung loosely near the butt of his gun. He faced Savage with a challenging stare. Savage stared back. Neither spoke.

The anxious onlookers waited. Their eyes shifted from the marshal to the cowboy, wondering who would be first to go for his gun.

Savage broke the silence.

"There's been enough killing," he said.

Castledine made no move.

Savage reached inside his shirt and brought out the leather pouch. He held it out toward Castledine.

"I came here to deliver this bag of gold, that's all."

He tossed the pouch onto Roan's lifeless body.

Castledine nodded, and his body relaxed. He strode to where his brother had fallen. He cradled Roan's body in his arms and carried it to Hezzy Thorne's funeral parlor.

The crowd began to disperse, quietly stirring about, questioning in hushed tones what had caused the commotion.

Out of the gathering waddled the fat, colorless mayor, accompanied by his gaggle of cronies who seemed always to be where the mayor was.

"Mr. Savage," the mayor squeaked.

Savage favored him with a wordless look.

"Mr. Savage," the mayor squeaked again. "When you came to town, folks hereabouts thought you were nothing more than a paid killer with a thirst for other people's blood." The cronies nodded agreement as their idol continued, "And all you have done since is to confirm our suspicions."

Savage's look told the mayor he had no interest in what he had to say.

But the mayor was not finished.

"We would appreciate it," he said, glancing about, seeking the approval of his witless entourage, "if you would depart our city without delay."

Savage offered the mayor a tolerant half-smile, regarding him with the same curiosity that he reserved for bugs. He turned to Amos at his elbow,

"Have you seen Meg?" he said.

Cully tossed a thumb over his shoulder to where the crowd had cleared away in front of the Last Dog Saloon.

"Over yonder," Amos said.

Savage looked past Cully's shoulder, and saw Meg staring at him. Her eyes scarcely cleared the tops of the batwing doors. She burst out the door, and bounded down the steps to the street where Will waited.

"I'm taking Amos with me to Junction City," he said. "I've got to go to Abilene and do some business with Judge Barker, then we'll be on our way."

"Judge Barker?"

"About Aubrey Roan. The judge has to know what took place here. There'll be time enough to talk about that when you come to Junction City."

"Am I coming to Junction City?"

"Didn't I tell you? There's a valley there that'll feed a whole herd of cows and a few folks. I was hoping you'd be one of them."

With a broad grin and a glance at Cully, she said, "Be damned, Savage!"

"I can't offer you much besides the land and the cows," Savage said. "That's all I've got. The catch is, I go with them."

"That's quite a speech, cowboy." She laid a hand on his arm. "Why did you tell me this now," she whispered, "in front of all these people?"

"Well, I guess I never thought—"

"I need to hug you and I can't. Charlie would be after me with a hickory stick for sure."

Savage spotted Charlie watching with a wide grin from the boardwalk.

"I'll send for you," Savage said, "as soon as we get settled."

"Can I bring Henry?"

"You bet. You bring Henry. And, Meg, will you see to Carrie's burying for me? I'll tell you about that when you come."

"You bet, Savage."

His gaze ambled past Meg and down the street to where Castledine was mounting his black stallion. They traded silent nods, then the marshal kneed his horse toward the jail, leading his dead brother's roan stallion.

Savage was anxious to hit the trail. He climbed into the saddle, and reined the bay toward Abilene. Amos fell in beside him.

At the end of the street where the prairie began, Amos turned for a final wave to Meg and Henry. Charlie Crum joined them in front of the Last Dog.

Savage put a spur to the bay. He could hardly wait to see the shocked look on Lester Hogan's face when he dropped the bag of gold on his desk.

He pulled up and looked back. Amos was still waving goodbye.

"Are you coming, Amos?"

Printed in the United States
216088BV00003B/6/P